SING ME TO SLEEP

A SERIES OF SACRILEGIOUS EVENTS NOVEL

R.M. VIRTUES

Created with Vellum

For the monsterfuckers

AUTHOR'S NOTE

Content warning: This novel includes descriptions of consensual non-consent, humiliation/degradation kink, sleep paralysis, explicit sex, rough sex, religious imagery, monster sex, monster appendages, depression, PTSD, past home invasion, prescription drug use, loss of a parent (past), on-page death, violence

1

PENELOPE

Mist and shadows. All she can see is mist and shadows. Both living, both breathing, neither welcoming in any sense of the word. The latter curls in on her like gnarled hands, yearning to touch, to taste, to torment. The former mutes all sound beyond her labored breaths, and labored breaths are the only thing willing to leave her lips despite her best efforts. She cannot see a thing. She can't even see her own feet beneath her, surrounded by fog and silence, both pressing in on her until they become a physical weight on her chest.

Something stirs behind her.

Run.

She listens to that voice in her head because that voice in her head is the only one who has offered to help, and she has no clue what else to do. She runs. She runs, and she keeps running, but for all she knows, she is going nowhere. The shadows close in, constrict around her until she's struggling for even the faintest breath. She opens her mouth, and it takes this as an invitation, crawling down her throat, shredding skin and muscle.

"No!" Her voice breaks at last, but it is long too late. "No, please! Please! No! No!"

Hands grip her shoulders, yanking her back. Now she remembers. She remembers what she was running from. She flails her limbs, kicking, screaming, fighting...

"Penelope! Penelope! Penelope, wake up!"

Another hard swing of her arm, and she just misses Jenna's face, her eyes snapping open on the end of a wail. She's - in her bedroom. She's back in her bedroom, her sheets tangled around her legs and sweat causing her hair and tank top to stick to her skin. Jenna's face is frozen in terror, her lips parted and her brown eyes bulging, her dark curls frazzled with sleep and panic. Judging by that look alone, you would think this was the first time she'd had to awaken her sister from such an endeavor. But no. It wasn't even the first time tonight.

"Hey, you're okay," Jenna manages with a heavy exhale. "You're alright."

Shock and confusion quickly morph into frustration, Penelope slapping her hands against the mattress.

"Fuck!"

"Hey, it's alright, P. It's okay."

Tell that to the bags under her eyes, the loss of appetite, of hair. Nothing had felt 'okay' or anything near it for the past six months. *Six months.* That's how long it had been since she'd slept through the night. Six months since the night terrors came and made a home behind her eyes, lurking in the shadows, waiting for her to rest. Or to try.

"You gotta take the pills, P," Jenna pleaded the way she'd done for the past several weeks. "Tonight, before I leave, just give them a try. They'll help. I know they will."

Penelope flopped back onto her pillows, screwing her eyes shut and immediately opening them again. Deprivation was not yet desperation, but it would be soon. She could not possibly go on like this much longer. She can barely get out of bed, and she can rarely go back to sleep. It was taking its toll.

"I don't want to take anymore pills, Jenna," she sighed.

"And I get that, but you are going to burn out."

"I *am* burnt out."

"Okay, listen to me." Jenna grabbed her shoulders, pulling her up into a sitting position. "Just try it once. If you still feel the same tomorrow, I promise to flush them myself. Please, Penny, I'm worried about you. Mom is worried about you. You're running on fumes, and it isn't healthy. I know I don't need to tell you that."

Penny chewed her lip, staring down at her hands. They were still trembling. She pressed her nails into her palms and squeezed until it ached. She had nothing else to say. They had said it all over the past few months. Jenna being right did not negate the depth of the struggle. Nor did the extent of her will and the excess of her exhaustion. Her sister simply couldn't understand. Nobody could. Because what happened had been the worst thing to ever happen to Penelope, and she had endured every second of it alone.

No, not alone, not entirely. And that was half the problem.

Four armed men. Four blood-curdling screams from her father echoing through the house. Four bullets embedded in the dry wall above the couch in the living room. Four minutes wrestling with the intruder that entered her bedroom. Four seconds that felt like four lifetimes holding her taser to his stomach. Forty-five minutes trapped in her own bathroom with nothing but the monotonous voice of a disinterested dispatcher in her ear. Forty-five minutes before she was told her father was gone. And now six months without sleep or any sense of peace. Six months of struggling to crawl out of bed anyway. Six months of regretting every breath she had taken since. She was beginning to lose sight of a point.

"Come on," Jenna urged. It wasn't that she didn't miss their dad. It was that she was much better at suppressing the urge to fall apart. Especially since she wasn't there. "Let's go get breakfast."

"I'm not hungry."

"Then you can watch me eat, but I'm getting you out of bed. We'll go out, get food, come back, and watch movies until it's time to take a pill and go to sleep. You can even sleep in my bed, so I can watch you."

"Seriously, Jenna?"

"Seriously. Now come on."

PENELOPE STARED at the bottle sat in front of her, her fingers tapping against the table's surface in an erratic pattern. *Deep breaths...Deep breaths.* She shut her eyes, the burn that came with not blinking merciless and antagonistic. She opened them again quickly.

She was exhausted.

She picked up the bottle, dragging the pad of her thumb across her name printed on the label. Her father's name. *Bardhan.* Jenna swore up and down that just half a tablet would give her the best night's sleep she'd ever had. While she had faith in her sister's claims, the thing was... Penelope wasn't sure she wanted to sleep anymore. Every time she closed her eyes, quite literally, all she could see was that outline, darker than the dark around it, hulking and harsh in the corner of her room. That figure had been there ever since, in the corner of her eye, watching, waiting, her father's screams permeating the air like a foul stench. What could possibly be more terrifying than that? Sleep was not the problem. What awaited her within it was.

"You have to sleep," Jenna commanded as she entered the kitchen. She was like a broken record. "I'm not lying to Mom anymore, and you know she will move in here for the next two weeks if she thinks she has to."

Nothing short of the truth, Penelope knew. Her mother had done that right after The Incident although it was just as much for her as it was for the girls. The only way she would allow the sisters to remain living on their own was if they agreed to move closer to her, and since Jenna's job was more remote than anything, they had agreed. And not at all reluctantly. Even if Penelope didn't want to hide beneath her mother's skirts, she did like the idea of all of them being closer.

"Really?" Penelope sighed, looking up at her sister. "You would tell on me?"

"To save you from ending up all Russian Sleep Experiment on me? In a heartbeat."

Penelope gathered her jet black hair and piled it atop her head in a messy bun, her bronze skin glistening with the aftermath of their face mask treatments. The spa treatment Jenna had insisted on hardly did anything to calm Penny's nerves, not when her sister was leaving her alone overnight for the first time since the incident. And not just overnight, but for two entire weeks.

She screwed off the cap, staring down at the light purple tablets within. The room seemed to hold its breath, waiting to see if she would give in or not. It made her uneasy, rolling her shoulders and stretching her neck with a hard swallow. Before she could slap the cap back on, Jenna reached into the bottle, extracting a single tablet and placing it on the table. She already had a knife in hand, and she used it to break the tablet in two, sliding one half to Penelope with an expectant look. Penelope stared up at her, mouth slightly agape and eyes blown wide. Fear crept up her throat - or was that bile? Maybe both. Sweat collected on her brow and the back of her neck while her mouth went dry. What would she see when she succumbed to sleep? Or more importantly, what would she fail to see?

"I'll be right there with you, Pen," Jenna assured her, brushing a hand over her hair.

"No, you won't," Penny said quietly, her eyes falling to the table. "You can't be."

"No. I'll be there to pull you out of it if I have to. And I will."

If there was one thing Jenna was willing to do, it was own her role as eldest daughter. She played Mom when Mom wasn't around, and she held Mom when Mom needed someone to hold her together. She had needed that a lot since she had sent her husband away for a weekend only to find out she would never see him again.

He had been visiting when the home invasion happened, he and Penelope waiting for Jenna to return from her work trip to Phoenix the next day. He'd fallen asleep on the couch, right there on the frontlines, mere hours after arriving. If Penelope had known it would be the last time she'd see him alive, she would have stayed up later. She would have stayed laying on the couch opposite him. She would've been with him. Whatever that would've meant, she didn't care. As long as she was with him. As long as he hadn't died alone.

She squeezed her eyes shut, hot tears spilling down her cheeks before she knew what was happening. Jenna was there then, wrapping her arms around Penny and pulling her tight to her chest.

"I know," she whispered. "I know, Pen, but I can't lose you too. I can't let you slip away from me."

Penelope could hear it in her sister's voice, the strain to be strong, the hurt that inhabited the darkest crevasses of her being. Jenna pressed a kiss into her hair, Penelope gripping the forearm around the front of her shoulders with a soft sob.

"Okay," she breathed. "I'll take it."

If she was lucky, it wouldn't be a stranger she met in the dark tonight. It would be her father, and if she had even a sliver of a chance to see him again, she would take it.

After a hot shower and a cup of tea, Penelope took half the tablet Jenna had cut for her and climbed into bed beside her sister. Jenna put on cartoons, something reminiscent of their childhood, and although Penelope groaned in embarrassment, she was secretly grateful for it. Anything to soothe her nerves and keep her calm as she anticipated the effects of the medication.

"What if it doesn't work?" The question left Penny's lips of its own volition.

"Then we'll try something else. Your therapist said that coping was a lot of trial and error, right?"

Penelope bit her lip, curling her fingers into the comforter. The words bounced around in her head, Belinda's voice a soulful and soothing sound. Truth be told, Penelope would be far worse off if she hadn't walked into the older woman's office just weeks after the home invasion which was a terrifying thought considering how run down she remained even now. Work, school, all of it had fallen to the wayside because she hadn't been able to cope. She had barely been able to breathe for the first two months, the panic attacks and paranoia ravaging her body like rabid animals. Now that she had sunken to the bottom of this pit, she wasn't sure she would ever be able to climb all the way out. Jenna never lost hope, but Penelope wasn't sure she'd ever had much to begin with. Her father was gone. How could the world have the audacity to move on after that? How could it all just keep going?

It happened slowly. The sound of the TV growing softer, the room fading to black, her grip on Jenna's hand loosening. No dreams, no memory of falling asleep; there was only the falling itself. It felt as though she had only blinked, and then she was waking up in her sister's bed. However, it was not yet morning. The room remained pitch black around them, a void she had to stare into until her eyes adjusted. Yet once they had, she wished they hadn't.

Her attention was immediately drawn to the corner. The shadows that painted it, they were - *alive*. And they —or it— had begun to grow. At an alarming rate.

And she couldn't move.

She strained against whatever invisible bonds pinned her to the mattress, but it was of no use. She could not move. Apart from the short range of motion of her head and the movement of her eyes, she was helpless. She could not even speak. And although Jenna remained beside her, she could not call to her, could not reach for her, could do nothing but lay there.

And the shadow was growing bigger.

Fear wrapped around her, urgent and unforgiving, clawing at her throat. There was no rational thought, no concrete contemplation that she could latch onto. Although she knew what she was seeing and feeling, it was as though her mind failed to accept it. In doing so, it prevented her from regaining control. All there was now was panic. Then...

Then the shadow started to grow smaller.

It was like she was zooming out of the frame, those shadows shrinking back into the corner until she could breathe again. Until she was freed from this nightmare of a prison. Or prison of a nightmare.

She bolted upright with a yelp, her breathing heavy and sweat slipping down her forehead. Jenna lay beside her sleeping soundly, pale blue light being sifted through the curtains. It was morning. She had slept through the night.

2

PENELOPE

"I'll check in when I get to the hotel."

Jenna entered the kitchen, placing her bags on the floor before gathering her purse and phone from the counter. Penelope had just finished washing the dinner dishes, wiping her hands on a hand towel before turning to face her sister. Jenna was already embracing her, and Penelope fought not to cry.

She had never felt so much like a lost child, and at 28, that was more shameful than anything. She tried to take pride in having made it through a whole night without waking up screaming, and Jenna supported her in that venture. Nonetheless, one good night was minuscule in a sea of so many bad ones, and "good" was a generous term for the feeling of being nailed to her bed while something lurked in the corner, but she had to conquer this. Some way, somehow, she had to figure it out on her own.

"I'll be fine," she assured Jenna. Or herself. "Don't worry."

"I will always worry. It's what I do, but I will worry less once I know you're actually sleeping."

"I *did* sleep."

She pulled back, giving Penelope a pointed look. "I mean consistently. Take the pill, P. I mean it."

"Okay, I will. I promise."

"And call if you need anything, no matter the time of day. If I don't answer, I will call you right back."

"You'll be working."

"I don't care. If you need me, I'll be there."

They hugged once more before Penelope walked Jenna out to where her rideshare was waiting to take her to the airport. Penelope tried not to think about the vast distance between here and Toronto, how impossible it would be for Jenna to rush back if something happened. Their mom only lived two streets away, but Zoya's brand of worry was a much more overwhelming thing, and Penny hated to make her worry. Because she would, and she would take great pride in doing so.

Waving from the driveway until the car disappeared beneath the oncoming dark, Penelope realized that a part of her, a very small part, had hoped she could tag along.

Deep breaths...Deep breaths.

Stilling herself, Penelope walked back inside, locking the door and arming the security system as she reminded herself they were in a gated community with round-the-clock security, and their neighbors weren't all white middle-class snobs who would turn the other cheek if a brown girl started shrieking in the dead of night. However, what could anyone do against her memories? And the terrors she conjured in her sleep?

Heading upstairs, she prepared herself a hot bubble bath, hoping to take some of the edge off, but the silence was as sharp as ever. This house was much larger than the house they had lived in before The Incident, but Jenna's tech firm had relations with the HOA in the area and when they heard what happened, her superiors had taken it upon themselves to handle new housing arrangements closer to Zoya.

Despite her being prime breadwinner at the moment, Jenna had insisted Penelope take the master bedroom, but Penelope supposed it was because she was home far more often. Jenna was constantly traveling, and while she had limited it during the past six months, it would have to start picking up again soon. Like now.

Turning the water off in the now filled tub, Penelope set the bottle of pills on the edge of it along with a glass of water before undressing. Slipping into the bath, she let out a slow sigh of relief, shutting her eyes for as long as her mind would allow before they popped back open and searched the room. Months ago, she had hoped that once they caught the guys who had come into her home and stolen her father, she would finally start to heal. Then they caught three out of the four of them, and nothing changed. She knew then that even if they caught the one that had been in her room, the one she had tased, it wouldn't matter. She would still be broken. Her father would still be gone.

She picked up the bottle once more, and she swore it grew heavier each time she did so. Jenna's voice echoed in her ears, a bittersweet event she hoped to carry through the week. She pushed down on the lid and twisted, flinching as if she expected it to explode in her grip. When it didn't, she peered inside at the tablets before dumping them in her hand until she found the other half of the one she took last night. After looking between it and the others though, she decided to try a full tablet. Maybe it would wipe out the remnants of her night terrors she had endured the night before. Maybe she could blink, and then it would be morning, and she would no longer feel drained.

She swallowed, or she tried to, but her throat was dry. Her eyes watered, anxiety pressing against her temples and making her head throb. For a moment, she tried to convince herself that it would be perfectly fine sleeping for only three hours every other night, tossing and turning throughout, waking up screaming at the top of her lungs until her vocal chords abandoned her too. But then Jenna's voice kept getting louder until she finally pushed the tablet between her lips and gulped down the glass of water, letting it carry the little pill out of her reach.

Setting the glass on the floor, she picked up her phone to put on some ambient sounds. There were several text notifications, two from her friend Naima and one from her friend Shane, but she didn't feel like answering them at the moment. Instead, she went for the other item in her toiletry basket.

The vibrator was small but strong, a sleek, pink little waterproof bullet that had done her more good than any therapy session thus far. It helped with the anxiety, giving her something else to focus on for at least the hour that its battery lasted. Flipping it on, she submerged it in the water between her thighs, resting her head back with a soft whimper as it found its target, sending a series of tremors through her willowy frame. She sunk deeper into the water, her eyes fluttering shut and her legs spreading open.

Before the home invasion, she had begun growing addicted to being alone, and that was because before the home invasion, her ex-boyfriend was her worst nightmare. Now, solitude was both a blessing and a curse, and she hated that some desperate strangers had been able to ruin it for her.

No. It would be hers again. It had to be.

Her chest tightened, back arching against the porcelain, the water sloshing against its sides. It always got her to her first orgasm so quickly, causing her toes to curl against the edge of the tub as she tried to muffle her moans. Once she vaguely remembered she was alone in the house, her sounds grew louder with unabashed passion, her free hand grasping the tub's edge. She was still wrestling with the aftermath of the first when the second orgasm began to build, the steam around her thickening. She gasped. She was close. So very close. So...

It came crashing down on her with merciless force, sweeping her up in a dizzy spell that had her lightheaded and overwhelmed. The steam wafted up through the air, surrounding her on all sides, pressing into her shoulders like hands. Down, down, down...

When she came to, the water was cold, and the vibrator had long gone quiet. Sleep had taken her with one whisk of its cold hands, and they clawed at her even now, making every part of her exceptionally heavy. Shock held her in place for a moment, and then... Then, it was something else.

She couldn't move. Again. Not her arms, not her legs, nothing. Well, okay, not nothing. She could move her eyes. The only thing she couldn't do with them was close them. It was then that she realized the light was off. She knew she hadn't turned it off, and she briefly hoped the power had gone out. Until she saw it.

It was there, in the corner, the way it had been the night before. And all those months ago in her bedroom when she awoke to her father's shouts. Darker than the dark around it, hulking and harsh. It grew larger as she watched, filling the room until its shadow reached across her face. Fear gripped her around the throat, making it difficult to breathe. She begged and pleaded with her fingers to work, for her legs to show mercy, for her mouth to be on her side. None of them listened. She kept struggling.

"Relax."

Penelope withered where she lay. The voice was like ice water and broken bones, stinging every inch of her before piercing skin and muscle. Then he materialized, not like the intruder who had entered her room but something else entirely. His skin was obsidian —or at least that was what it looked like against the lighter shade of night behind him—his eyes a blood red and his - horns? No, his antlers. Large antlers, not like a ram or those cartoon demons but like - like a massive elk.

The points of them were sharp, so sharp that Penelope was convinced she could break skin just by reaching for them. They were black too with swirls of ivory and gold wrapped around the roots, and they flashed across the air like lightning bolts, spreading through the space. Then he was smiling, and her thoughts were washed out by the sight. His teeth were bright white, the tops sharper than those on the bottom, not overly large but not entirely human. His tongue unfurled over his thick bottom lip, reaching well beneath his chin even as it curled upward. Her vision blurred beneath the welling of her tears, and she quickly tried to blink them away. He reached for her cheek, his palm hovering so close that she could feel the vibrant heat rolling off of him. He never made contact though. Somehow, that felt worse.

"I'm nothing to be afraid of, Penny." A sigh. "Not anymore."

He moved like smoke, his edges unfocused even once she was able to rid her vision of tears. He was massive, eclipsing every inch of the bathroom. It hardly helped him in his cause, which was to say it didn't help at all. Relaxing was the last thing she was able to do. And yet...

There was something about him, something that called to her, something that softened the initial shock of his appearance. Something that made her *want* to believe him. And really, what choice did she have?

"I'll protect you from the bad things." His eyes were as vibrant as flames in the dark. "Just understand that you are *mine*."

She managed to whimper again, looking away from him. Or trying to. He hissed, not in an angry way but in a... soothing way?

"You are safer than you have ever been." Despite him whispering the words, his voice seemed to come from everywhere. "You have all the control here. You just have to trust yourself. Trust yourself, and nothing can ever harm you again."

What did he mean? What was he talking about? How could that be true when she couldn't even fucking move! He seemed to be reading her every thought, clicking his tongue as he moved closer to her. Then his face was no more than a few inches from hers, and the air in her lungs began to chill.

"I'll prove it to you." His breath ghosted over her lips. "You want me gone, just say the word."

What word! She screamed it at him in her mind, convinced he could hear it or read it or take an educated guess of it. She continued to scream it until he smiled again, this time with a look of sympathy. Then, a word.

He didn't say it. He didn't say anything else. But it flashed across her conscious mind, there and then gone in the blink of an eye. Not that she could count it that way. She chased it nonetheless, grasping it between her teeth for only a moment. Her eyes screwed shut, her lungs filling with air, and then she was moving all at once.

She fell out of the tub, yanking a towel down from the rack with her before using the sink to help her up. The light was on again. Or it had always been on. She checked the room nonetheless. It all felt too real to be a dream. *He*, whoever he was, felt too real.

But there was no sign or symbol or clue to his existence that confirmed her belief nor was there anything to completely reject the conclusion either. She was trembling so bad that she struggled to secure the towel around her waist, ripping the door open and peering into her bedroom. It was light outside, so bright that she had to squint against the sun streaming through the blinds. It halted her in her tracks momentarily before she turned back around and went to scoop up her phone. It was dead of course, which would account for the lack of music as well now that she remembered she had fallen asleep to it. How long had she been out?

The pill had yet again done half its job at least. She'd slept, but she certainly wouldn't call it the most peaceful sleep she'd ever had. And she certainly wasn't ready to tally another "good night".

3

PENELOPE

"You were paralyzed?!"

Jenna's voice pierced her eardrum at the highest possible pitch, aggravating Penelope's pulsing migraine. She quickly pulled the phone away from her ear.

"I mean, I think?"

Penelope's eyes were still fixed on her laptop screen before her, the grotesque creature displayed upon it staring back at her with challenge in its eyes. It wasn't him. Or it. Or whatever that was she had dreamed or seen or both or neither. However, it was the closest she had come so far after scrolling images upon images of night terrors for three hours.

"Are you okay?" Jenna asked, her voice slow but still dripping with worry.

Oddly enough, Penelope felt fine... Or maybe not fine, but certainly not afraid, not like she was after The Incident. If anything, she was more - angry? Yes, angry. Angry that her sleep was being tampered with, angry that she couldn't just have one night of rest, and angry that whatever it was that haunted her now had taken such a horrific shape, a shape that was not that of her father.

Yet somehow, she felt like the creature was easier to manage than a human intruder, and not just because only one of them had actually hurt her. The monsters were already real. As for the creature, she had no clue what he was, not yet, but he was nothing compared to the men that lurked in the corner of her eye at all times. They had already done more damage than any creature could.

She had never experienced sleep paralysis before, but according to what she'd read thus far, it wasn't at all discriminatory in its visitation schedule. It was actually quite common, and the solutions seemed simple, but Penelope didn't expect her case to be anything of the sort. There was no real formal treatment for it, and it had been reduced to nothing more than a disruption in one's sleep cycle. That hardly helped considering all she knew were disruptions in her sleep cycle, and what was one more when the rest seemed so set in stone?

There were of course a number of remedies and tips from other people online who had experienced it, but none of them truly seemed to be foolproof, and her head was starting to hurt. She supposed she would just try the easiest one and lay on her stomach tonight regardless of whether she took the pills or not. The fact of the matter was that it hardly mattered at all. It was either sleep paralysis or night terrors, and thus far, one had been far worse than the other. Scary as he may have been, the creature hadn't yet hurt her. As for the night terrors? They opened up her deepest wounds every single time they visited.

"I'm fine, Jenna," she huffed at last, shutting her laptop and pushing her hair from her face. "Listen, I'll talk to you later. I'm gonna go take something for this headache and make something for dinner."

"Are you sure? I have a few more minutes. I can stay on."

"No, it's fine. I have to get used to being on my own."

"Yes, but not after what just happened!"

"Look, if I can get through this and have the guts to sleep tonight, I can get through anything."

Jenna was quiet for a moment, and Penelope could picture her stark white teeth chewing on her mauve-painted lip, the wheels in her head speeding up their pace.

"Okay," she conceded at last. "You're fine, and I'm fine, and I'll call you when I get back to the hotel."

"Okay, sounds good."

Penelope hung up before Jenna could ask one more time if she was okay and stood from the counter. She had slept until half past noon, and scary entity aside, she did feel more rested than she had in weeks. Maybe that was why she was so calm now, numb to both the image of the creature and memory of the break-in. It almost scared her how distant that memory seemed. It seemed too easy, as if reality was just lurking behind a curtain or door waiting for her to let her guard down. She refused to play hide and seek with it though. For now, she would savor this small sliver of comfort.

She had just put a pan of lasagna in the oven when her phone rang, the tone letting her know it was Shane. She had been texting him earlier after finally responding to his message from the night before, and he was the one that told her to look up sleep paralysis, but she had forgotten to text him back once she fell down the rabbit hole. She hadn't mentioned the creature, only the inability to move, but the initial search had eventually led her to where she needed to be.

"Hey, sorry, I got caught up on my - research," she informed him once she had the phone pinned between shoulder and ear. "And now I'm making dinner."

"You got room for one more?"

"What? You're gonna come all the way out here?"

He lived at the southern edge of the city, which was at least a 45-minute drive to her house, and she would hate for him to feel obligated. He had been there for her in every way he could be since the week after The Incident when she finally started accepting communication again, but she didn't wish to become a burden to him too.

"I'm already outside," he stated proudly. "I got a present for you."

"Outside? Seriously?"

"Yeah, I figured if you didn't answer, I'd just leave it on your doorstep and shoot you a text."

"You're unbelievable."

"Yeah, well, reward me with dinner."

The doorbell rang as soon as she set the phone back down, and she rushed over to open it. Shane stood in the doorway, his wavy brown hair pushed back and his dark green eyes gleaming with mirth. He ran track back in college, and that was evident in his thick calves and slender frame, his pale skin taut over his toned muscles. She was certain he still ran. In fact, she didn't think he could live without it.

"What did you bring me?" She questioned as he sat down at the table.

He smirked and revealed a shiny green envelope from behind his back, handing it to her. She took it with a raised brow, pulling open the zipped top of the pouch and peering inside.

"Weed edibles," he informed her, stepping inside and

pushing the door closed behind him. "I got you a chocolate bar, some gummy bears, and - a lollipop, I think? Maybe? Enough to get you through the week."

"Weed? I don't think I should be getting high with everything going on."

"Listen, it's all Indica strain. It's lights out with these, so just take somethin' before bed tonight instead of that pill. Those tranqs fuck with you chemically, you know? But my sister told me when she had sleep paralysis, she started smoking heavy right before bed, and it helped her. I don't have any scientific data or anything, and this is purely anecdotal—"

"Shane, please." A runner who minored in psychology for fun. She chuckled and shrugged her shoulders. "What if I trip or get paranoid or something?"

"If you want, I can sleep on the couch, stay up while it kicks in."

"Oh, you don't have to do that. This is more than enough."

He placed a hand on her shoulder. "Hey, I want to. If this will help, I wanna see it through. I'm worried about you, P. You were looking rough last time."

"Oh, thanks."

They both laughed, and he patted her back before dropping his hand. "I'm just sayin'. You look good today though, so maybe the night wasn't entirely bad."

"I do feel rested, you're right, but - I don't know if I ever wanna sleep again after that."

That was what she had been too afraid to tell her sister earlier. Though now that she said it, she wasn't sure that was entirely true. She was beginning to understand what that conflicting feeling was that took root in her belly each time she revisited the night prior. It was curiosity.

"Let's just try it, alright?" His voice drew her from her thoughts. "If it doesn't work, at least I'll be here to keep you company on your all-nighter."

The truth was that as much as she didn't want to be alone, she also didn't want company, but she decided that trying the weed wasn't the worst idea. She couldn't evade sleep forever, and if this got her out of taking those pills when Jenna got back, she was all for it.

"Alright."

He grinned. "Perfect! Now what's for dinner?"

She rolled her eyes but started setting the table for two, pushing the thought of bedtime from her mind for the time being. Or at least to the back of it. While they ate, Shane talked about his new job doing cybersecurity for some very important firm while he saved up for grad school, and Penelope told him what it was like living in a gated community and preparing for her master's track in the fall in spite of the rampant depressive episodes. Regardless of her earlier opposition to it, it felt good to have company, and Shane was a solid conversationalist. They had a lot in common, and he was a good guy. However, when he'd asked her out right after graduation, she'd said no, and she still stood by it.

She couldn't say why for certain. It was more than just having left her ex after years trapped in a nightmare. There was just something off. Or maybe - missing. While he may have had a chip on his shoulder she couldn't quite comprehend, Shane was perfect on paper. He came from money, and now that he had secured a job in cybersecurity, he was bringing in a good chunk of his own. There were times where he seemed to be so far ahead of everyone else, not just financially but mentally, running towards the horizon without realizing how much of the scenery he was passing up. Still, he was the dictionary definition of stability as was his family. He was a safe choice, the *safest* possible choice, and he was going to make his wife very happy. But Penny had never really been known for making safe choices, and even if The Incident had managed to change that, dating was also the furthest possible thing from her mind.

"Have I told you that you're an amazing cook?" he asked around a mouth full of lasagna.

She laughed. "Even if you had, I wouldn't tire of hearing it. This is probably the most ambitious thing I've cooked in a while too although I didn't make the sauce the way I - used to."

"It's perfect. If you just send me two trays of this for Christmas, I would be happy."

She rolled her eyes. "Okay, now you're exaggerating."

"Why would I? This is what, my third serving? I don't need to. Besides, it's a much better present than I was gonna get you for your birthday next month."

"Oh, no. You're not getting me anything for my birthday."

"And who's gonna stop me?"

"Shane..."

"No, come on, seriously. Check this out. I won't even leave you in suspense."

"Yes, because you're shit at keeping secrets."

He smirked, pulling out his phone and tapping the screen a few times before he turned it to face her. She leaned closer to see, and her stomach flipped. It was a watch with a narrow black band and a silver face that looked blue in the light if you held it just right. She knew this because she used to have this exact one. Her father had given it to her.

She swallowed hard, looking down at her food.

"What's wrong?" he questioned, putting his phone

down. "You don't like it? I mean, truly that's why I wanted to show you. I wanted to make sure I got you something you would like, so—"

"No, no, it's not that. It's just - how did you know?"

She looked up at him. He looked confused.

"Know what?"

"I - I had that watch." She gestured towards him. "I - my father gave it to me, but it - they took it in the..."

She couldn't finish the sentence, shaking her head. Shane hissed.

"Shit, Penny, I'm sorry. I just - I saw it downtown, and I thought it was really pretty, so I wanted to get it for you. I can definitely pick something else, or—"

"It's okay. I just - I don't know. It just caught me off guard."

"Hey, don't worry. I may be shit at keeping secrets, but I can pick gifts just fine. For the most part. I'll find you something else, something almost as good. I got you."

She tried to offer him a smile, appreciative of the sentiment. It wasn't his fault. How could he possibly know it was the exact same one? She rarely wore it, instead keeping it on display on her bedside table back in the old house. It wasn't because she didn't like it but because she was so afraid of losing it. Her father had given it to her at her high school graduation just before she started college with one of his signature witty dad jokes inscribed on the card. *Something to remind you how quickly time flies when you're having fun!*

Damn, she missed him.

Shane respected her silence, but eventually, she was able to stir up a conversation again, not wanting him to feel bad about the coincidence. Once they had cleaned the kitchen, they sat down in her room to watch a movie, each of them taking one of the smaller gummy bear edibles to ease her into what Shane called a "premier bedtime high". They were about halfway through the rom com she had chosen when she started to feel the effects, a low buzzing sliding over her brain like a sheet and making her feel light and warm.

She'd smoked before, but that was long ago when all you really had was the choice of a pipe, bong, or rolly as a means of intake. Her therapist had mentioned the suggestion early on in their sessions, but at the time, Penelope could admit that she really wasn't all that interested in healing. She wanted to mourn, to be angry, to be absolutely unbearable. But most of all, she wanted to suffer, to pay penance for letting her father down, for leaving him to fight —to die— alone.

Sleep took her without her permission once again, and although she knew she had fallen asleep on her stomach, when she awoke, she was staring up at the ceiling. Her room was still dark, like well past midnight dark, and yet she was still able to make out the shadow cast across the room. It was almost as though it was laying over her chest, its weight settling atop her like another blanket. Or the lid of a coffin.

She fought against the restraint, struggling until her head throbbed with the exertion. Nothing gave. Nothing loosened. Nothing came to her rescue. Her body refused to listen, to heed her pleas. It simply sank deeper into the mattress until she was all but fused to the frame. Then there was - *something.* It spread over her line of sight. And then kept spreading. Like a darker shadow. Like a bottomless abyss.

No.

Like wings.

Great black wings were stretching out right before her eyes, and between them grew another black mass. It was him, the creature or demon or whatever. She could see him clearer now than the night before, his vast antlers glinting and his red eyes trained on her. She knew before she even tried to scream that she couldn't, and once again, her body betrayed her, glued to the bed with no hope for help. She wondered if Shane was still awake, if he would check on her soon, if it would matter. There was no way he could see what she saw, and even if he woke her up or pulled her out, she would still see this thing when she closed her eyes. Part of her wished he had stayed in the bed beside her now.

And another part of her? It wanted to know what this creature wanted.

"Having a sleepover?"

His long tongue flicked out around the question mark, his large head tilting to the side. She realized then that he was perched on the footboard of her bed like a large bird, and maybe it would be funny or endearing or something if she weren't colored in with fear. So no, not like a large bird, not right now. More like a gargoyle.

"Not of the sexy variety, I see." He seemed to take a large whiff of the air. "That's good. But you didn't touch yourself before bed tonight. Was that because of him? Or because of me?"

He was reading her thoughts again. But - of course he was, right? He was all in her head. *It's just a dream. It's just a dream. It's just a dream—*

His breath caressed her jaw. "If I'm just a dream, why won't you let me touch you?"

The question cut through her like an arrow, embedding in her chest and threatening to break apart at any moment like shrapnel.

"I understand," he cooed. "You *should* be afraid of me. And I *should* want you to be. It's wired into your system, into mine. It's an instinct. The problem is that *my* wires seem to have gotten crossed. Your fear is not the delicacy I wish to indulge in. It is a bad batch. Just the thought of it makes me ill. I do not want your fear, Penelope. I want your peace. I want your pleasure."

He lofted a hand, flashing her his palm before he moved it towards her belly. However, it again would not touch down. He made no contact, and she was beginning to wonder if he could.

"I am your monster. Make of me what you will."

His eyes bore into hers, vibrant and vicious, hypnotizing her so that she forgot for a moment that she was helpless. And - she believed him. Every word he said, she believed him, and she had no sort of resistance available to throw up in the wake of that realization. Her fear tore from her grip, and it felt like she had just forfeited her last ounce of control.

His hand touched down against her belly.

"And you are *mine*."

Warmth radiated from the point of contact, coursing through her entire body and permeating her blood like gasoline. The growl he emitted at the sensation of her skin was the match he dropped into it, setting her alight. Her body continued to betray her, terror licking away at her insides until it began to taste that hint of rebellion, and once it did, it morphed into something else entirely.

An unknown object drifted along her ankle, then her calf, dipping beneath the fabric of her sleep shorts and teasing the skin of her inner thigh. Her body refused to obey her, but it had no issue obeying him, shivering beneath whatever touch he was bestowing upon her. Then suddenly, her back was arching and her eyes were rolling back. The thing that had been touching her now wrapped around the heated flesh of her wrist, and her mind was filled with a montage of lewd images, images of her. And of him. Her body contorted in pleasure, her neck flushed with heat, her legs propped on his shoulders, his tongue disappearing between her thighs...

She forced her eyes open again, shaking her head and throwing him a bewildered look. He was no longer perched on the footboard. He was sitting right next to her, and he was smirking.

"I could do it for you if you'd like," he hissed. "Any of those things. *All* of those things. I am your monster, Penelope. I can do whatever you need me to do for you, to you. I can soothe every fear and frustration you have ever had. I can make sleep enjoyable again."

She was struggling to focus, to think, to find her fear. Her lungs stuttered with short breaths, and she knew without seeing that her face was flushed. This had to be a dream, one dirty and demented and threading right through her nightmares. She could not let herself get lost in this.

He moved his face closer. "I know you liked what you saw in my little movie. I can smell it all over you. I know what you need. That's my job, to know, and I do. I know very well that all you really need right now is for me to go down there and feast on that pretty little cunt of yours. Then you'll see that I am much better suited to your pleasure than your pain."

He brushed his thick fingers against her jaw, the claw of his thumb scraping down her throat. It was so soft, so cautious, she shivered again, a long breath pushing its way out of her lungs. Her body relaxed of its own volition, arching toward his touch despite the terror rising in her throat once more. Or trying to at least.

"You can talk if you wanted to, Penelope." She watched

as his wings folded into his back, making him seem suddenly so much smaller. Or at least closer to average. She was almost grateful. "You can do anything you want to really. You just have to trust yourself. I told you that."

She wanted to. Of course she wanted to, but she couldn't!

"Yes, you can," he insisted. "You did it last night, remember? You chased me away. No hard feelings of course. This is all very brand new, but I can assure you it gets easier. And if you can't trust you, then trust me. I haven't hurt you yet, have I?"

She stared up at him, eyes wide, new questions forming and fading in quick succession. She knew better than anyone that this was always subject to change. She hadn't seen him angry, unnerved, disappointed. However, she was judging him by the standards of men. He was anything but.

"I will never let anything happen to you. I can't. You've ruined me for it."

The words wafted between them like a thick cloud of smoke, obscuring her vision and filling her lungs, and… she believed them. Again. She believed him again.

But how? Why?

Still, certainly not enough to let him *do* anything to her, no matter how alluring that little magic movie he put on was. No matter how curious she was about whatever remained wrapped around her wrist. No matter how his breath felt on her neck…

She turned her face from him, only just missing the touch of his mouth so that it skimmed her cheek. Heat bloomed there, but she pushed it away, berating her body for its endless betrayal.

"You want me to stop? You want me to go away?" The words stung like salt in an open sore. "You know what you have to say, Penelope, but understand. I can only touch you if you want me to, if you invite me to, so if you didn't..."

He gripped her chin, pulling her face towards his and forcing her to meet his bottomless gaze. His tongue flicked out between his lips, the end of it disappearing from view. Then she felt it dragging up along her throat, tracing the path of the moan she failed to suppress. It was a guttural thing that cared nothing for the boundaries of her paralysis, and he devoured it eagerly.

"Say my name," he challenged again. "You have all the power to summon me or send me away, at any moment. Just say my name." His large hand slipped down her front to tease the hem of her shorts. "Or I could make you say it."

Screwing her eyes shut, she began wrestling with it again, the knowledge of his name, because despite the determination of her denial, something was tickling the back of her throat, flitting across her thoughts like a butterfly. Or a stray bullet. And then she remembered the night before, the word she had chased right before he disappeared, the one she knew and then didn't know from one breath to the next. It was... It was...

"Acheron!"

Her eyes popped open as her voice echoed back at her. The room was lightening, the sun beginning to rise, her hands struggling against nothing more than the sheets they were tangled in, but she was alone. She was alone, and she was lonely, and regret stung her in all the places once bound to the bed. Her demon was gone. *Acheron*. She thought it over and over. She said it again. Why wasn't he coming?

And why did she want him to?

4

PENELOPE

Penelope's phone screen lit up on the table before her yet again, but she made no move to answer it. Instead, she continued to gnaw on her thumbnail, her eyes darting back to the bag of gummy bears sitting just beyond her phone.

*You have **every** right. This is what **everyone** wanted. This is what **you** need.*

She had been doing this for the past two hours, having landed there after walking Shane out to his truck and re-arming the security system. He had offered to stay longer, to go into work late, to lay down with her, to make her breakfast, but she had rejected each and every offer. What she really wanted was... well, what she really wanted scared her, so she hadn't outright admitted it to herself yet.

She kept seeing him in the corner of her eye, his broad wings and chiseled body, his serpentine tongue and his massive hands, his majestic antlers and his roguish smile. But each time she looked, he was gone, and no matter how many times she uttered his name, he refused to properly manifest.

Fuck, she really was losing it, wasn't she? Sitting here in her kitchen summoning some horny demon after finally getting a little bit of sleep. What was wrong with her?

Then again, was he not the reason she had been able to sleep? She still believed he was being honest when he said he wouldn't hurt her, but she needed a reason for that trust, and she could not for the life of her commit to one. Even if all of this was in her head, what good would it be to grow attached to a dream? And how long before it —*he*— turned back into a nightmare?

Her mother was calling again. Penelope knew if she didn't answer, Zoya would continue to do so. Then she would call Jenna, and then Jenna would call worried, and it would just be best to get it over with. Accepting the call, she put the phone to her ear.

"Hey, Mom."

The first thing she heard was a sigh of relief. "How are you? Are you alright?"

"I'm doing alright, all things considered."

"Are you sleeping? Jenna said she got you some pills to help while she's gone, but if you need me to go over—"

"You don't have to do that, Mom, I promise. I - I slept really well last night actually."

"Did you?" Which actually meant 'are you lying to me?', but Penelope wasn't, not now.

"I did, really, but - I didn't take the pills. Shane got me some edibles from the dispensary, and it helped."

Zoya sucked her teeth. "See, I told Jenna to try weed before she went and got you on those pills. Far fewer side effects, and they're less likely to get in the way of your other medications."

"That's just what she knows." Penelope assumed that meant Jenna hadn't told her about the night before last.

"The point is I slept, and -" She glanced at the gummy bears once more. "I think I'm gonna go do some more of it right now."

Her mom nearly squealed. "Yes, you definitely do that. Get all the rest you can. I'll call you later, yes? And we can get together for dinner at some point this week. I love you."

"Okay, Mom, I love you too."

Hanging up the phone, she set it back down as her eyes fell upon the bag of gummy bears once more. With each passing second, the urge grew stronger, the urge to succumb, to return.

Acheron. Acheron.

She had hoped his name held the same power when she was awake as when she was asleep, and while she had abandoned questioning her own rationale, she still wondered what other mistakes she might be prone to making if summoning a demon was now something she was fully invested in doing. What would happen if she were to release him from her dreams? Would he still care about hurting her then?

For now, she supposed it was indeed best to go to *him*. Especially now that she knew how to leave.

Picking up her phone and the gummies, she marched back upstairs, dumping the items on her bed after she'd locked herself in her room. It was nearing noon now, but once she closed the blinds completely, that was irrelevant. She had to go back to sleep. She had to know if it had been real, if *he* had been real, and she had to know right now.

Taking two gummy bears out of the bag, she tossed them both into her mouth, chewing quickly and swallowing. Acutely aware of Shane's warning about a delayed high, Penelope struggled to keep calm as anxiety and impatience brewed beneath her skin. She glared at the corner of her room, waiting for the dark mass to appear and grow into a vast body with expansive wings and sharp horns and dark eyes. It never came.

Laying back against her pillows with a sigh, she looked up at the ceiling, She willed the weed to hit faster, to let her seep into the mattress and meld into whatever world Acheron inhabited when she was awake. She recalled the shape of his mouth and the cut of his claws and the weight of his hand on her belly. If she closed her eyes, she could feel his breath on her neck again. If she closed her eyes, she could admit to herself she had wanted him to do whatever he wanted with her because being careful had never gotten her anywhere and being reckless might just give her some reprieve.

Though the longer the weed took to hit, the more she second guessed her decision. Maybe she just needed to get off. She hadn't been able to with Shane in the room the night before, and she had grown used to doing it each night before bed. She imagined kisses on her neck, hands in her panties, fingers in her pussy. She imagined all those possibilities Acheron had shown her. She imagined demanding them of him.

She dipped a hand into her shorts without thinking, gently stroking the outline of her folds through her panties. She bit down on her lip with a muffled groan, the skin more sensitive than it usually was despite Acheron being unable to reach it before she sent him away. She pictured what would have happened if he had touched her there. Would he have marveled at the moisture already collecting between her thighs? She was pretty damn wet when she woke up, so she could only imagine she had been so in her dream or his realm or whatever. And all because he'd touched her once.

The thought of his reaction had her pressing down on her clit until her hips bucked, a whimper clawing its way out of her mouth. She pushed her free hand beneath her shirt, palming a breast and twisting the nipple until it pebbled between her fingers. Heat rushed through every inch of her, and she struggled not to call out his name now. Shoving her shorts and underwear down her thighs, she slid her digits through her folds, hooking them over the edge of her entrance as her thumb massaged her clit. She was too invested to stop and seek out a toy, far too eager to touch and perfectly capable of handling herself with the thoughts swimming around in her head. There was no reason to break her current concentration and disrupt the image manifesting behind her eyes, despite how hard that image struggled to do him justice.

She could not believe how much she wanted to be touched by him, realizing that the fear had not subsided but simply morphed into something else, stitching itself along her desire and dressing itself up as need. She fought off the shock, instead giving herself over to the sensation. Anything was better than the forlorn grief she had been carrying all these months. Whatever Acheron had done to her, he had given her something new to feel. Hunger. Hope. The joy of having something to look forward to. He had done more for her in a night than counselors and cops and everything in between had been able to do for her since the incident. There had to be something to that. Even if he was just inside her head, his influence was palpable, and she needed it. It may be the only thing she could trust in now.

She didn't know if she'd cum. She didn't even know she'd fallen asleep until her eyes fluttered open again and she was unable to move. Her hands had returned to her sides, and she was vaguely aware that her shorts were still bunched around her knees, panties tight around her thighs. However, the bulk of her focus was planted on the dark and shadowy cavern of her bedroom and the growing mass in the corner of her eye. There was no fear to be found now. It was stifled behind so much else. She felt - desperate or anxious or impatient or maybe a combination of them all. She need not wait long. Soon enough, he stood there before her, swelled to his full size with a proud grin on his face.

"You figured it out," he barked with a raucous laugh.

She hadn't expected such a sound from a demon. It spiraled through her like a corkscrew in a bottleneck, touching down in the pit of her belly and making her skin tingle. She offered him what she hoped was an apologetic look, her tongue pressing into the roof of her mouth but her lips failing to fall in line.

"You're back quick." His eyes flashed with a sudden curiosity, sharpened to a point and aimed right at her pride. "Did you miss me?"

She could only stare at him although for the first time, she felt grateful that she couldn't respond. She wasn't about to tell him the truth, and she was too afraid to try and sell him a lie. Judging by the look in his crimson eyes, she would say he already knew regardless. He always did, right? He could read those thoughts before her tongue ever acknowledged them. Before she could squirrel them away.

He ran his hand up her leg, trailing alongside it so that he could stand level with her hips. In one swift wave of that hand, the blankets flew off of her, exposing her bare cunt to the open air. Her mouth snapped open, and although no sound came out, she could feel the scream hooking into the wall of her throat. Acheron took a deep breath through his nose, straining his neck towards her... He was sniffing the air.

His eyes seemed to glow, the muscles beneath his black flesh flexing and bulging. His antlers seemed to grow outward, the golden tinsel that adorned them winking at her in the dark.

"You were thinking of me, weren't you?"

She wasn't sure if she meant to or if she had committed to the movement at all. All she knew was that she felt her head shake from left to right, and then he was laughing.

"You want me to touch you and find out?"

She shook her head again, but her mind was shrieking its pleas, begging for a brush or a tease. Without warning, one thick finger swam through her folds, the very edge of his nail carving out the path before it until it could trace the rim of her entrance.

"You dirty, filthy girl," he growled, the descriptors reverberating through her bones. "You fell asleep thinking about it, what I showed you. That's why you came back so soon, isn't it?"

Another shake of her head, but it was more for show than anything. It meant nothing to either of them anymore.

"Remember what I said. If you didn't want me to touch you, I wouldn't be permitted to. You want me to stop?" He slid a single finger into her heat, and her eyes snapped shut, her body shuddering violently. "Prove it."

She couldn't. He knew it, and he knew that she knew it, and more importantly, she didn't want to. She had no explanation, no rationale. All she knew was that she wanted him to keep touching her, and all she had to do was let him.

He squatted down beside her as he probed her with his digit, curling it against her walls and thoroughly massaging them. She was burning up from the inside, her eyes rolling back and her mouth molded around her silent moans. She could feel his gaze on her, cataloguing her reactions with each and every touch he was merciful enough to grant her. Then his mouth was against her breast, tonguing her nipple through the fabric until it hardened between his teeth, and if she could scream, she certainly would be wailing. Everything felt so much more potent in paralysis, ironic as it was. She had expected to feel nothing, but instead, she felt *everything*. Every brush of his lashes, every graze of his breath, every swirl of his tongue, every sensation and emotion bottled up within her and fixing to burst the first chance it got.

"Didn't get to finish, huh?"

He'd pulled back, and he was now gripping a handful of her shirt in his free hand. With one swift yank, he freed the garment from her body in one piece, tossing it behind him. Then he inserted a second finger into her cunt, spreading both of them apart and stretching her out around the sheer girth of them. If those were his fingers, she could not imagine how large his cock was. He had to have one, right? Hell, even if he only had his fingers to use, he still wasn't lacking. He knew how to use them, and use them well. Maybe too well.

And really what she was fantasizing about was that long, thick tongue of his.

"Oh, don't worry, you'll get that too," he smirked, snagging the thought from her mind like fruit off of the forbidden tree and biting straight into it. "This is all you needed to start sleeping again, isn't it? A reason?" She licked her lips. "Don't worry, Princess. I'll make sure you never miss another wink of sleep again."

So many questions revolving around logistics and limitations flitted across her mind, but she was nowhere near coherent enough to offer any of them. Instead, she let herself sink deeper into the moment, and he seemed willing to allow it, refraining from picking those questions too and answering them aloud. He was far too focused on watching his fingers plunge in and out of her anyway, twisting and curling them, driving her towards the orgasm she hadn't been able to reach on her own and touching places she couldn't have reached either.

His other hand returned to her breasts, kneading them in his vast palm. His claws must have receded some because they hardly scraped her skin, and when she managed to get a glimpse, they looked much shorter than they had the first time she saw them, like human nails rather than predator's talons. And all while everything else looked so much larger.

He added a third finger.

It had barely slipped into her when she came, her body straining against its invisible bindings in a shallow arch. He pressed down on her chest, pinning her back down, every inch of her trembling in place. He withdrew his fingers, and she watched in silent awe as he sucked them into his mouth, his eyes going completely black for several long seconds before they were glowing again, a brilliant scarlet. She screwed her own shut, unable to handle how devastating he looked while tasting her. However, when she opened them again, he was no longer standing beside her. No, he was hovering several inches above her, his wings outstretched and his horns bent back.

He moved away, down her body, landing on his knees between her thighs. She would have spread them wide open had she been able to. He moved them apart himself regardless. She swore the bed had grown longer, long enough to accommodate his gargantuan frame so that he could brace his heels against the footboard. She watched his horns bow together, cautious and considerate, their sharp points no longer a threat to her guts once he lowered his large head. She watched his tongue unfurl from his lips, disappearing between her thighs the way it had in his collage, and she shivered, yearning to feel it against her folds.

"Greedy girl," he teased, his voice crowding around her. "It didn't take long, did it? For you to give into me, to yourself. You wanted it bad, didn't you, you filthy little slut?" She whimpered. "You've wanted this tongue inside of you since you saw it. You want me to clean up this mess you've made, don't you? Let's see you take it then."

His callout was just enough of a distraction for her to be caught off guard by the sudden drag of his tongue along her slit, curling just beneath her clit and giving it a firm flick.

Please please please—

It was the only word she knew apart from his name, which she was doing everything in her power *NOT* to say at the moment. He started slow, tempting and tantalizing, tracing the seam of her lips again and again until her thighs were all but vibrating around his head. Only then did he shove his tongue into her. Only then could she move.

Her hands came up before she knew what was happening, taking hold of the two thick trunks of his antlers.

"No!" She shrieked, the word bouncing off of every surface in the room. "No! Don't—"

Yes! This was the word that echoed in her head, drowning out the first as she dragged him closer. His tongue swelled inside of her, elongating well past where his fingers had reached and stretching her to his will. She ground her hips up into his face, feeling the cut of his teeth against her skin and the strong grip of his hands as he scooped up her ass. Secretly —although probably not that secretly at all— she hoped he left a mark, something she could wake up to in order to prove that it was real, that *he* was real, and it was more than some beginner's luck in lucid dreaming. She wanted to remember—

"Ah! Fuck!"

I can promise you this, Princess. This is something you'll never forget.

He hadn't removed his mouth from her heat nor his tongue from within it, but still his voice surrounded her, invaded her. Again, it was as if it was coming from everywhere, rattling around in her head like a song she couldn't stop singing.

Her heels dug into his broad shoulders when something touched down on her clit, vibrating mercilessly against it. Lifting her head, she looked down to see a smooth, black object shaped like a diamond with a long black cord extending from it. That cord was attached to him... Wait, no. Not a cord. A tail. *His* tail.

You'll certainly lose count of all the ways I can make you cum.

She gripped his horns tighter, pulling him closer, deeper, until he was all but welded to her body. This pleasure was unlike any other pleasure she had ever experienced, clawing at her core and planting something there that she would never be able to root out. She was once more certain this had to be a dream. No type of real being could possibly deliver this much pleasure, each and every second overflowing with euphoria. She was no longer chasing release. No, it was chasing her.

Cum on my fucking tongue. We both know you want to, dirty girl.

It was like flipping a switch. She came again, her sharp cries clashing with the loud and lewd slurping sounds he was making as he feasted on the fruits of his labor. The end of his tail was now vibrating at an alarming rate, the sound similar to that of a rattlesnake. She yanked hard on his antlers, but he hardly budged, which had her coming up off of the mattress with cries turning to sobs of overwhelming pleasure. His name crested her lips, and before she could scramble for the reins, it was permeating the air in a blood-curdling scream, every syllable enunciated and echoing through her ribcage. The last thing she saw was his serpentine tongue withdrawing from her folds, the dark skin around his mouth glistening, her juices dripping off his curled lips.

Her eyes snapped wide, her throat burning with the strain. Still, she cried out for him. But the room was empty. He was gone, and she was awake.

Maybe that was for the best.

Yet as she sat up in bed, she let out a sharp hiss, looking down at her nude body. There, on her inner thigh, was a blood red symbol carved into the skin. A mark. *His* mark.

5

PENELOPE

"Do you need me to come over again tonight? I'll bring dinner this time."

Penelope chewed on her thumbnail mindlessly, staring off into space and only vaguely hearing Shane's question through the phone. Despite that, she was quite aware of how excited he sounded, but she wasn't interested in playing host tonight. She was only interested in how early was too early to go to bed.

What an odd turn of the tide.

"No, it's alright," she said softly.

"—Are you sure? I'm still in the city, so it's not a long drive. I could be there in fifteen minutes tops. I was gonna stop for Chinese food anyway."

"I appreciate that, but since you helped me finally get some sleep, I'm - looking forward to doing it again." She laughed nervously, hating to disappoint him. "I'll be fine."

"Well, I'm glad I could help. We didn't finish that movie though, you know? It was a good one."

"Oh, yeah, maybe some other time."

She could make out the sigh he expelled, guilt tickling

her stomach. However, it was nothing compared to the anticipation needling into every inch of her skin, most notably her inner thighs. She was about to cut the call short and evade any further insistence when he spoke again.

"So - you heard from the cops again?"

She froze, taking the question carefully in her hands like a sharp blade. Or a loaded gun. Then, shifting uncomfortably in her seat, she swallowed hard.

"No. I - I haven't."

Not for weeks now. Before the first arrest, they called every now and again to update her on the case, but since catching intruder #3, there had been no updates. Plus, out of the three they'd caught, none of them were talking. The exception was the call she received just to confirm she had been reimbursed by her insurance for the items the men had managed to steal. Jewelry, money from her father both in the form of cash and his card and PIN, and most of the sisters' electronics. As for the money Jenna and Penny had hoarded in the house for emergencies, that was long gone because apparently if you keep $3,000 in cash in your house, whatever happens to it is on you. Especially when no one should have known where it was.

The insurance money had come much quicker than she had expected, and she had let Jenna handle it completely. It felt far too much like blood money to her. Her father had written that check with his last breath, trying to stave off these men who had valued property over human life.

She shut her eyes, fighting off a sudden wave of nausea.

"I'm gonna call it a night soon, and I need to clean up the kitchen, so I'll talk to you later, yeah?"

"Oh, uh, yeah. If you - you wanted to call me when you get into bed, I don't mind staying on the phone 'til you fall asleep."

She was growing irritated, perhaps irrationally so, but she did not care. It was almost dark outside. That meant it was late enough to wind down, take a few hits off the vape pen she had ordered from the dispensary and get in bed.

"That's alright, Shane. Good night."

She hung up without waiting for a response, reaching for the remote beside her and shutting off the TV before she stood from the living room couch. She double checked the alarm system, ensuring it was armed before she went into the kitchen and put away the leftover tuna salad she had thrown together for a late dinner. Anticipation grew into a palpable excitement, one she failed to hide, even —or especially— from herself. She couldn't deny it. She couldn't stop thinking about *him*.

And in all that thinking, what she had come to realize, to her great surprise, was that he made her feel safe. To some extent, that was the beginning and the end of it. When he was touching her, she knew in her marrow that she was as safe as she could ever possibly be, even from the things that lurked here in the waking world. It felt as though he had etched the assurance within her bones.

These feelings weren't in spite of his appearance either. If anything, the look of him only added to that trust. More than that, it fueled her hunger.

From the regal wings to the bizarrely long tongue to the versatile tail —and all the things he was able to do to her with them— she was absolutely enthralled by the sight of him, and each time she closed her eyes, it was all she could see.

Yet it still wasn't close enough, and no matter how many times she uttered his name under her breath, he remained nothing more than a memory. She was beginning to think that maybe, she was losing touch with reality, that he was some sort of coping mechanism her subconscious mind had drawn up out of sheer desperation and lack of sleep. Though even if that were true, the fact of the matter remained. She wanted him. And he was an overly effective coping mechanism.

Picking up her pajamas, she changed swiftly into her dark tank top and red sleep shorts, tying her hair up in a loose bun. She had considered ditching the pajamas altogether, or at least swapping them for something more alluring, but she decided that would ruin the game. This game he had her eager to continue. Why, she wasn't sure. After The Incident, it was difficult to believe she could even *pretend* to say no to him, to let him continue regardless, to let him take her by force. Yet the mere thought stoked a flame in her belly, the fear she had once felt now wrapped in unbridled desire. It was as though the two were intertwined, and with him, one needed the other.

Besides, the intruder had never touched her, never gotten the chance, and even now, she was convinced that he would have just let her remain asleep if her father's shouts hadn't roused her. Not that it mattered either way. Acheron was no part of that nightmare. He was a dream all his own, and coping mechanism or not, Acheron as a shield and Acheron as a lover were also two separate entities, neither influenced by the other. And it was because she felt so safe with him that she was able to play this game in the first place. He just knew his way around her body. It was almost as if he'd been there before.

Fuck, that tongue.

Climbing into bed, vape in hand, she took a few long drags until the harsh coughing in the aftermath became too much, searing her throat along the way. She set the pen on the nightstand, snatching up her phone and opening an ebook to read. Though the one she had started recently was highly enjoyable, that hunger clawed at her stomach. Taking her lip between her teeth, she exited out of it and instead searched for something a bit more *generous*.

Finding a highly rated erotica was not all that hard to do. She opened one and immediately began skimming for the more racy bits. The description of the couple hardly mattered because she could only picture one pair, and her skin buzzed with the exhilaration of it. She lay on her back eagerly now, fumbling around in her dresser drawer for a vibrator. She pulled out a silicon purple one with sucking motion for her clit, the reminder that she had yet to see his cock inadvertent and pervasive. Considering his size, not just of his overall form but of his fingers and tongue and even the end of his tail, she could only imagine what it was he had in store for her.

She shivered and bucked her hips as soon as the toy touched down between her thighs, which were already slick with arousal and firm on the conclusion that this would not suffice. Still, she swirled the head eagerly, pressing it every now and again hard against her nub, her moans and whimpers like a prayer. A prayer to a demon. *Her* demon.

She took her time, dragging it out and torturing herself for the sake of suspense. The weed had her gliding through open space. Stars glittered behind her eyes, and her clothes seemed to grow tighter. She lay there on the edge, her thoughts a collage of Acheron and his versatile appendages, the thrill getting her higher than the weed ever could. Yes, she was addicted to the recklessness, the loss of control, the unbridled chaos that came with running headfirst into danger. Because despite that loss of control, this was still a choice, *her* choice. It meant she still held the pen and pad. She could still write her own story and refuse to submit to the one her trauma was attempting to scrawl out on her skin. It didn't matter if the demon was real or not. He was *hers*. And he had made her feel alive for the first time in months, perhaps even more alive than she'd ever been.

Sleep wrapped around her limbs like chains, reeling her down into the depths of its realm. She let her phone fall beside her, careless as to whether she needed to charge it or not. She'd turned off the ringer, unwilling to be interrupted in the midst of Acheron's visit. She would not waste a second of it. She refused.

The toy was still buzzing, background music that lulled her further into slumber. She breathed out slowly, the tension draining from her body. She could almost feel his approach, his breath on her jaw, his tongue in her pussy, his hands on her ass, his sharp voice. Terrifying indeed, in the most arousing way, and she could not wait to see how he reacted to her current state, how he would laugh when she tried to deny she was thinking of him, how he would humiliate her with his filthy tongue and callous confrontations, how he would surround her in those moments before she could remember how to move. She wanted him to take her, and she didn't want him to be gentle about it. She wanted him to do so like the monster she had believed him to be.

Something yanked the comforter from her body.

Her eyes were slow to slide open halfway, hooded with sleep and lust alike. She need not wait for him to manifest. He was already standing beside the bed, the comforter clutched in his large hand.

"Were you being a bad girl?"

The growl seemed to take over for the toy no longer pinned against her clit, sending jolt after delicious jolt through her folds. He swept his tongue over his lip, her eyes trailing after the movement.

"I asked you a question, Penelope. Were you being a bad girl?"

She shook her head on instinct, arms stuck to the mattress and mouth dry and deactivated.

"Oh, you're a liar now too, huh?"

He ran a hand up her thigh, his fingers hesitating a moment before they touched down. He was checking to see if he could touch her, if she consented to that touch. And oh, did she.

She attempted to catch a glimpse of what he had between his own thighs, but it was too dark, everything below his waist blending in with the blackness of her room. In fact, it hardly looked like her room. It just looked like empty space. Not that she cared. As long as he was there, everything else was inconsequential.

She strained her neck as he delivered a sharp and merciless slap to her sensitive pussy. The sting went straight through her, throbbing in her throat.

"Then what's this?"

He held up two thick digits, her arousal webbed between them. He reached down and applied it to her lips like a gloss before shoving his fingers into her mouth. She fought not to bite down, but after a moment, thought better of it. He seemed to anticipate the change of heart however because the moment teeth touched rough skin, he pressed down hard on the back of her tongue until she gagged. Then he plunged them deeper.

"Mm, you better learn to take these fingers because soon you're gonna have to take my cock in that pretty little mouth soon, and compared to that? This is nothing."

She was sweating, the sheets already dampening beneath her. The thought had her squirming in place, and if he wasn't prying her mouth open further, she would have tried to cry out. She looked up to meet his fire red eyes. They narrowed at her. Then he smirked.

"Oh, you wanna see it, don't you? What a filthy little slut you've been, Penny. Getting off to the thought of it, huh? You really think you can handle it?"

It was instinctive, the quick shake of her head, her gaze pleading. He barked a laugh. Then his fingers were out of her mouth, and he was giving her folds another slap. This one was harder, louder, but it seemed to knock loose the lump in her throat that neutralized her vocal chords because an equally sharp cry ricocheted around the room, and it only took one look at him to know she had been the one to make it.

"There's my girl." She shivered, back arching slightly at the phrase. "Punishment is still eminent, but I might not drag it out as long as I had planned too."

He took hold of her chin with his other hand now, squeezing hard enough to bruise.

"You know what you gotta do to send me away, to go back to your cold sheets and your little toy. I will respect it, but you have to say it, or else I am going to do a lot of very nasty things to you and your tight little holes, Penelope. I am going to wear you down to nothing. I will earn your tears and demand your cries. I will open you up and take everything from you, so you better use that mouth of yours." He pulled her lower lip down. "Before I do."

"No."

It was the faintest whimper, her throat already hoarse. His teeth glinted in the darkness, his eyes burning above them like lit candlesticks. Fear was in fact present, but it remained entangled with her need, the thought of what he might do eating away at her patience.

"No? What do you mean no?"

"No!" Stronger now but still barely more than a squeak. "Stop."

"Make me stop. You know what you have to do."

"Please."

His hand whipped across her clit again, a sob racing from her lips.

"You're gonna learn today what happens when you lie to me." His hand moved from her face to her throat, easily encircling the column and giving it a rough squeeze. "And unless you send me away, I will not let you leave this place until you've learned it properly."

Then he was moving again, rising up into the air, his wings extended. Up close, she could make out the most intricate details of the design. They were not quite bat wings, but they also weren't quite bird wings either. It was more like a mixture of both. They looked silky like feathers but rough like skin. Before she could analyze them further though, he had straddled her chest, and that glimpse she had tried to catch earlier was paid in full.

HIs cock rose up before her, longer than long and thicker than thick, the bulbous head level with her lips. She suspected it could reach her forehead just fine if he wanted it to judging by the versatility of his tongue. Her eyes could hardly process the sight, a large obsidian obelisk adorned in defined ridges and deep grooves. The head was painted white already, his balls heavy against her breasts. All she could do was stare as he took hold of the shaft, stroking it at a sluggish pace with his eyes fixed on hers.

"This is what you want, isn't it, you little slut? Admit it."

She shook her head, and immediately there was another strike to her pussy lips, tears streaking down her face into the pillow beneath her. It wasn't his hand however. He was now gripping his cock with both. Then she saw his tail rise up at his shoulder, and it was almost as though it were staring at her. Like a viper prepared to attack. The end of it looked much bigger, wider than last night, and she gritted her teeth.

"Still wanna lie, huh?"

"No! I'm not lying! I don't - I don't want it! I don't!"

"Then why are the sheets soaked, Penelope? Why is your mind so fixated on it? Why could I smell your desperation before you arrived?" He leaned down, nearly bent double, grabbing hold of her face none too gently. His claws sunk into her cheeks. They grew wetter. She doubted it was tears.

"You wanna be my little slut, don't you?"

"No!" *Yes! Yes!* Another merciless slap. "No! Stop!" And another. She bit her tongue.

"You're gonna be."

"I'm not!"

"I'm gonna use you like one. I'm gonna fill every single one of your tight little holes with my seed. Even when you do wake up, you won't be able to get out of bed. You'll be worn down and exhausted, and you'll end up right back here where I fuck your brains out all over again. Is that what you want?"

She turned her face away from him. He dragged his tongue up along its side. His lips grazed the shell of her ear. His voice filled both her and the room.

"I'm going to ruin you, Penelope. I'm going to burn you to ash and then eat them. —But for now..."

He straightened up, shoving her head back down onto the bed before he was stroking his cock again, his tail resting against her clit, unmoving. She was still paralyzed and pinned down, but she wasn't complaining. At least not internally. Every word, every touch, every tease had her bursting into flame over and over, an endless cycle. He knew exactly what to say, exactly where to go, exactly how to make her squirm. He was drawing her darkest desires to the surface, her mind painting vivid pictures of the lewd and ludicrous, a wonderland of debauchery being constructed behind her eyes. She wanted it. All of it. She did not care if it hurt. In fact, she wanted it to.

"Your punishment. You're going to watch me cum on your face and then on your tits, and maybe, if you're a good girl, I'll play with your cunt. But only if you're a good girl. Understand."

"No! I won't!"

"We'll see."

He wasn't at all boring about this little show either. He gyrated his hips, soon fucking his hand, his shaft swelling until she swore it would eclipse her vision entirely. She shuddered at the thought of him shoving that inside of her pussy without warning, taking advantage of every hole he could just as he'd said.

He let his head fall back amidst a string of grunts and snarls, his antlers appearing to droop down like hair although the points remained aimed away from her body. She watched as cum began to leak from his tip, one hand back around her throat as he leaned forward a bit. Then his tail was moving, whether on purpose or on instinct, and she clenched every muscle she could. She was already so close to cumming just by watching him. His tongue hung down before him. If he wanted, he could wrap that around his cock too. Before she could envision it however, her body bucked and arched. He'd shoved his tail straight into her pussy.

"Open your mouth."

She was lightheaded and dizzy with the shock of it, her eyes hooded and her jaw tight. It took so much energy to shake her head, the vaguest 'no' crawling from her lips. He tightened his grip on her throat. She choked and gasped.

"I said open your fucking mouth. Do not make me do it for you."

Her pussy constricted around his tail as she fought for more power in her voice. "No! I won't! Hurt me, you fucking bastard! Do it!"

An image flashed across her mind, vivid but fleeting. His hand was whipping across her face. It played out in slow motion. Then his eyes were piercing hers, a question there.

Even now, he wanted permission. Right now, she would let him do anything.

She growled. "You can't, can you!"

His hand was heavy, coming straight off his dick to crack against her cheek. Somehow, it was exactly as hard as she wanted it to be, or needed it to be, as if she had guided it across her face herself. She could taste the blood before she could feel any pain, but rather than simply compound her fear, it seized her desire and began to squeeze it like his hand squeezed her neck. Like it was trying to drain it.

Before she could think of a response, he was smacking her lips. Not with his hand but with the massive head of his cock. His cum filled the crevice between her lips then he was yanking her chin down, opening her mouth. Immediately a salty sweet taste that teetered between ice cold and burning hot painted her tongue, which he slapped with his cock several times once he was able. She could tell right away that he could never fit that into her mouth, not at the size it was now.

"Don't worry," he grunted, no doubt reading that thought. "You won't get that privilege today. Not when you come here with the audacity to lie to me about that needy little cunt of yours."

As if to punctuate the sentence, his tail curled, and then it was vibrating. It was vibrating harder than it had last night. Her vision went white then black, a million stars bursting and dying before her. She was squirting, the sheets beneath her soaked in her orgasm. Then came the cries, feral and wild and not entirely recognizable as her own. He was doing it. He was ruining her.

"All that evidence, and you want to tell me lies, Penelope? Why can't you just admit you're a dirty little whore who wants nothing more than for me to use her like she uses her toys?"

She was only just coming down when his tail was retracted, but before she could miss the sensation, he was forcing it slowly into her ass. A louder cry left her, and she writhed beneath him. Then she was pleading and begging as if driven to it, as if he were pulling her strings like a puppet.

"No! No, please! No, stop! Stop it! Stop it!"

He pumped his cock faster, his tail twisting and curling until the entire tip, now the familiar shape of her little bullet, was buried inside of her ass. She kept pleading, kept demanding he stop even when she wanted him to do anything but. She fought against her bonds until her arms at last broke free, but even as she flailed them against his broad chest, he didn't stop. He didn't even slow down. He simply shoved his tail deeper and reached down with the hand that had been on her throat, tweaking her nipples with a harsh touch. She shrieked. He jacked off faster, a low growl rattling in his chest. Then, without warning, a fountain of white hot cum landed against her skin with a hiss, steam wafting up into the air. It felt like candle wax. Although it didn't harden, thick globs landing on her face and dripping down her cheeks, her forehead. Once she was masked in it, he stood up and over her, aiming that big cock down and pumping even faster, so fast that she could hardly make out his hand on the shaft. Then he was painting her tits in it, coating her body with reckless abandon. Just like he'd promised.

She came again without so much as a flash of warning.

His cackling filled the air. "Look at you. All I have to do is cum on you, and you're wetting the bed. Pathetic."

He withdrew his tail from her ass, but by then, she was nothing but a convulsing heap on the bed, his voice a million miles away. Vaguely, she wondered what happened if she were to fall asleep while she was...already asleep.

The thought alone drew her back to him, not yet ready to go, to leave her demon again.

He licked his lips, admiring his work before he lowered himself once more.

"Look, I can be gracious. I'll let you clean it up."

He shoved his cock towards her mouth. She jerked her head away. He snagged her chin again, turning her towards him.

"I said clean it up."

He hardly raised his voice. Still, it boomed around her, through her, rattling her bones and poisoning her blood and tickling her in all the places she was so eager to let him touch. She opened her mouth, and he immediately shoved the tip in, only the tip, but it was more than enough. Then he waited, allowing her to suck the head clean. The moment she had, he took that from her too, leaving her worn out but wanting all the same.

"I know you are. I know you want me to fuck you straight through the floor. So..." He brushed a finger down her jaw. "Maybe tomorrow, you'll come prepared to tell the truth."

6

ACHERON

Hell wasn't all fire and brimstone, at least not in Abyssus where the demons dwelled. It was the kind of dark utopia so many wanderers woke up and drew or wrote about in their stories. Buildings were constructed from black and red stone, every brick as shiny and sleek as polished steel. Some of them towered so high that the top was not visible from the ground, and others were of a more average size. The latter were often reserved for mortal souls who had earned a place away from the torment and torture of The Fires, working the businesses frequented by other mortals who were able to pass freely between realms. They were either bound to a demon or they had given their soul to a reaper, offering themselves the purest form of freedom at the highest of costs.

The city was surrounded by endless forests and dark woods, bogs and swamps and everything in between, all smoldering over plains of ash and bone. Beyond that lay The Peaks, vast ice mountains that encircled their city compound. Those lands was overrun with beasts of the most grotesque designs, ones no mortal could possibly hope to dream up even in their worst nightmares. Luckily. The Puri, the seven archdemons and architects of Hell, had a habit of reaching into the darkest parts of their mind and bringing whatever they found to life. Acheron's creator, Belphegor, was one of those seven and had given them the means to bring them all to life and make them impenetrable forces of security. Those creatures never entered the city, but if a mortal soul ever managed to escape the fires, they would find themselves in a whole new world of fear and terror. That fear would fuel the city, and that soul would never think to escape again.

The sky was a blood red, clouds of ash hovering high above the ground. They expelled their contents over the scorched earth like a soft snow every now and again, coloring the ground a rough grey. Acheron found it all beautiful. He had never wanted for anything outside of what home could provide. Until now. Until Penelope.

He could feel her even now, her anxiety, her anticipation, all working through him like the sweetest poison. How is it that he could miss her so deeply after only hours apart? This was no common occurrence. Demons had grown fond of mortals before. They had grown possessive, hungry, and horny for them too. That was all to be expected from those who championed the freedom of the self. However, Acheron had never heard of a demon who had fallen —and so gently too—for a mortal. It felt impossible. Worse than that, it felt dangerous.

"Where the hell have you been?"

Acheron glanced over his shoulder, halting his steps when he saw Xaphan gliding towards him, his great black wings stretched taut. He was draped in wolf fur, which was wet with the remnants of melted ice and actual snow. He had been north in The Peaks.

Xaphan was a Son of Lucifer and a leader of the reapers, so he spent his time collecting souls as opposed to tormenting their dreams. Like Acheron, he was also one of the eldest demons in Hell behind the The Puri, and apart from The Puri, he was the only being Acheron trusted with his life and had never tried to lie to. Xaphan ate lies for breakfast. And for lunch? The tongues that passed them.

"Working," Acheron returned with a smirk as the other demon landed beside him.

Xaphan's large black wings folded in, disappearing into his broad back beneath a swath of reddish black skin. The fur began to fade as well, his body adapting to the warmer climate of the central city.

"Working, huh? Thought you lot were losing wanderers."

He grinned, unable to contain his excitement. "I've found one. Which is why I've been staying close. I don't want to lose her."

Which wasn't entirely a lie. In fact, it wasn't a lie at all. As of late, with the growing interference from above, wanderers were in fact much harder to come by, especially those who came deep enough into the realm to be touched, consenting or not. And there were far less wanderers that consented to being touched, *ever*. That was another reason this connection with Penelope was so bizarre. In all of his centuries with the Somni Dae, he had only ever gained permission once, and he had used it against the mortal to harvest the maximum amount of fear. But all this was neither here nor there when it came to Penelope. He wasn't enamored with her due to convenience or desperation. Something in her called to him, and although her consent had come quickly, the thought of exploiting it hadn't even occurred to him. His touch was reserved only for her pleasure, never her pain. Somehow, that fed him plenty.

But that was not what he was meant to do. The Somni Dae had always had one motivation and one motivation alone. While other demons reaped souls and collected favors, sleep demons fed on the fear that drifted through their realm from the waking world like a pungent stench. It was the thrill of coming upon the strongest souls in their most vulnerable state, sleep creating a sizable chasm between body and spirit. Many were able to live their entire lives with a sturdy tether between the two, unable to be meddled with too much. But many others became wanderers due to some sense of limitation in the waking world, eager to venture out into a wilderness they could only reach in their wildest dreams. Or nightmares.

"I hope not too close," Xaphan warned, his tone dark. "Rafael and his little sprites keep trying to play boogeyman, and just because they're foolish doesn't mean they can't land a hit every once in awhile."

"I'll be careful. She wanders deeper than any soul I've seen, right into our realm. They can't touch us here. Plus, this one, she's worth all the risks."

Every single one of them too, but Acheron would always be cautious. After The Dominion began interfering with their work, wanderers were doubly protected by the veil that acted as a stern boundary between this realm and the waking realm, one they couldn't accidentally pass through the way they often had before and one demons were not allowed to manipulate or even approach in any way. This forced sleep demons to siphon small bits of fear that hardly sustained them much less Hell's quota. Still, every now and again, new wanderers would manage to create a path of their own prior to The Dominion locating them, and if they acted fast, sleep demons could use that path to reach them. Acheron couldn't be certain whether the archangels were aware of Penelope yet, but it didn't matter. It was too late for them to cordon her off now. It would take far more than a veil to keep her from him. Or him from her.

It didn't mean they wouldn't try.

Xaphan clicked his tongue. "She sounds lovely. Shame those fucking parasites are always trying to get in the way."

"Yeah, well, what else are they to do? The mortals are growing wiser, more alert. They've stopped looking to the sky and started looking in the mirror."

"Yes, and the Puri called it from the start, which is why we are all here now. Just because they outlived their faulty business model does not mean they should come try and stomp on ours."

"As if they know anything else."

Xaphan snorted. "Why would they? You get told you're perfectly faultless your entire existence, you'll eventually believe the lie, and then you'll waste the rest of your time telling everyone and everything else they are anything but."

"What does Lucifer say?"

"You know he never says much of anything, but Baal... He says to wait, to be patient. I can't imagine things have gotten all that bad yet when he's still up there running his brewery."

"Yeah, Bel and the others are still going up there too, business as usual."

"All I know is that something's happening, something they don't want us to know about."

Acheron shook his head, but he couldn't deny the reality. Things were changing, few of them for the better, and they had to be prepared for anything. Bel, who always had his head buried beneath his mounds of archives and stacks of scrolls, had always warned them that the reckoning would come. He just never specified what it might look like.

"If that's the case, we'll all find out eventually. No clash is ever quiet."

"Ain't that the truth." Xaphan sighed, running a hand over his curved horn. "This is where I leave you. I gotta go check in with the others. Heading back to your wanderer yet?"

Acheron looked up at the sky, the onyx moon sinking slowly towards the horizon. "Yeah, soon. I have a bit of time before she heads to bed."

"Have fun."

With a grin, Xaphan clapped a hand on his shoulder with a firm nod before diverging from the road, turning towards the eastern end of the city where his reapers held communion in their claimed pub. Acheron continued south, taking his time as he watched the moon sink lower and lower. Once it touched down on the horizon, darkness would radiate from it and paint the sky black, a canvas for the ashen clouds above. The Reapers of the Anima Dae would head up into the waking world, the Favors of the Crucis Dae would run off to claim their crossroads, and the Somni Dae would remain here, behind the veil. And all of them would have to do everything in their power to go unnoticed by The Dominion.

Stepping inside of his chambers, he shut the doors and locked them with a deep sigh of relief. Passing the time had become crucial to being away from Penelope. It had been four days since he'd first tasted her, three since he'd cum all over her face, and he'd been doing nothing but teasing her ever since. He knew what she wanted, but it was still so bizarrely intoxicating that she wanted anything from him at all, and he wished to savor it, to ensure she kept coming back.

She was staying in his realm longer, and last night, she hadn't even sent him away. Her conscious mind had pulled her from his hands, taking her back to the waking world to live a life unburdened by nightmares. They had yet to say more than a few words to one another outside of the filthy whispers and snarled commands, but he could sense her desire to start asking questions. It wasn't that he feared answering. It was that he feared what it might mean.

He turned to face his room, which mirrored hers in everything but life. In here, behind the veil, the world was grey, dulled and desaturated to the point of vague definition around him. He sat on the edge of the bed where their worlds would soon overlap, resting his hand against the lavender sheets. They weren't lavender here, but they were to her, and so they would be to him as well. He could feel her warmth. She was in bed. She was coming back to him.

Heat swept through him, the distinct drive of desire fresh on his tongue. He would wait no longer. Tonight, he would take from her all that she had been trying to offer him, and he would feel no shame for it. Nor would he ever return it. She would be his. He would possess her in every way she could be possessed without submitting her soul, and then he would remind her of it every night after.

He didn't bother waiting in the corner anymore, allowing her to gather her bearings before he made his presence known. Instead, he watched as his hand was slowly separated from the mattress, a solid mass materializing before him. He shut his eyes, her scent growing stronger around him. Then his hand rested against solid...skin. No fabric, just bare skin, rising and falling with each breath. Then a shudder, fear and desire filling the air in equal measure. Just like he liked it. He could serve his purpose and serve himself all at once. He could have it all.

"Doing the work for me now, are we?" He smirked, dragging a claw down her stomach. "And here I thought you didn't want all those dirty, filthy things I did to you. Isn't that what you said? Isn't that what you always say?"

Her jaw clenched, brown eyes widening when he pressed his palm into the valley of her breasts. She was beautiful, her jet black hair framing the rich brown skin of her face. Her mouth, the shape of it, made something in him ache. He wanted to know them, their taste and texture and how they felt on his skin, but that was a far more dangerous game, one he was not yet prepared to gamble on.

"Lie to me again," he hissed, his back straightening. "Tell me you didn't want that."

"I didn't," she forced out breathlessly, shutting her eyes. She was regaining her voice much quicker each night, and he had to admit — he was proud. "I didn't. I don't!"

"You're a liar, Penelope. A filthy little liar."

"I don't want it! I don't want *you*!"

Hunger roared within him, pounding against his ribcage and threatening to crack it wide open. She played this game as well as anyone. And as much as he wanted to protect her, he also wanted to break her.

"You could have said my name at any time. You could say it now. You got your voice back, didn't you?"

He gave her time to do it too. He always gave her time. She never did it. Not anymore. Still, he asked. And he would keep asking. If only to be sure.

"So use it now if you don't want this."

He wrapped his tail around her ankles, flipping her over onto her stomach. A strangled yelp met his ears. He rewarded it with the sharp slap of his hand against her ass.

"I don't!" she shouted. "I - I can't. It's too... You're too... It won't—"

He chuckled. "Oh, is that your only concern? The concern of a filthy little whore? It's whatever I need it to be, Princess, but rest assured. I'm gonna push you to your limits."

"No..."

"I'm going to make you scream."

"No!"

"And no one is going to hear you."

"God—"

He leaned over her, his mouth on her ear. "God is the last person you should be asking for help."

Her heart pounded in his ears, her blood a roaring river just beneath her skin. He could almost taste the tang of it on the air, his long tongue sweeping down her spine and between her asscheeks. Her fingers twitched at her sides, but she remained fixed to the bed. His own scraped lower, lower until it could slip between her thighs and curl against the edge of her pussy. The skin there was already slick.

Your cunt says otherwise, Penny. The truth is all over it.

He pressed the words into her mind, letting them linger long after she began to squirm and whimper. He curled his tongue harder, spreading her open as he knelt between her legs. Her fear amped up, her desire like a long howl, and he devoured them both with gluttonous desperation. His eyes rolled back, both of them hitting him like the hardest drug, and before he could rein it in, he was slamming his hard cock into her cunt. She hit a note that was well out of human earshot. He wished to put that song on repeat.

7

PENELOPE

Penelope knew she was screaming. She wasn't sure if she was screaming out loud or in her head. She only knew that she was. Acheron filled her twice over, his cock hard and thick and long. The grooves and ridges she had been inspecting for the past few nights were evident with each stroke, grinding and massaging and stimulating her walls each time he slammed into her aching cunt. He swelled and pulsed inside of her, preventing any inch of her from going untouched, unscathed. Keeping her pinned with a large hand between her shoulder blades, he used his other hand to spread her open further.

You want this, don't you? The words boomed inside her mind and through the room. *Don't you!*

"No!" *Yes*. "No, I don't! You - disgust me!"

"Then say it!" He said this aloud, sliding his hand up to the back of her neck and squeezing it hard. "Say my fucking name!"

The helpless shouts, the futile struggle, the empty insults — every single one of her efforts was a fluke that only served to get her exactly what she wanted. She had been silently begging and pleading for him to fuck her, *really* fuck her, to let her experience that monstrous cock inside of her. And time after time, he had denied her, demanded she work for it although she had no idea how or when she would fulfill the qualification. And tonight, he had taken her completely off guard although she suspected it was more about his impatience and less about any actual standard she may have met. Not that she was complaining. She didn't care why he was finally filling her up. She only cared that he continue to do so. And she could admit it to herself now. The only thing she wanted more than him taking her by surprise was him taking her by force.

And he'd given her both.

She bounced between intense pleasure and subtle pain like a tennis ball, his shaft stretching her further and further in every direction. Then, again without warning, he was invading her ass with his thumb... No. With his *tongue*, and something between a gasp and a sob escaped her. It expanded and narrowed in quick succession the deeper it went, her eyes rolling back into her skull so far that she swore she could see right through her head.

"You could if you wanted to." His words filtered around them. "You could watch me destroy every one of your little holes. I know you want to, you little slut. You want to file them away for later when you have to get yourself off, rubbing this pussy all over one of your pillows, humping one of your pathetic toys, fingering yourself and wishing it was me. But it will never be like this. It will never be enough."

Then his tail was against her clit, circling and probing, and any hope of doing something beyond laying there was lost. Even if she could move by now, she hadn't the mind to do so, much less the energy to try. She shrunk in on herself, wave after vast wave tossing her around until she was drowning in her own delicious pleasure. Her screams were lodged in her throat, allowing her to listen to his steady grunts and growled obscenities and the lecherous sound of his hips clapping against hers. He hadn't lied. He was going to ruin her.

Or maybe he already had. Either way, if she could, she would certainly thank him for it.

Overstimulation was an understatement, but each time she considered tapping out, he would hit another spot she had never known existed before, and she would lean into it yet again. There were mere minutes between orgasms, and she knew that if she were awake, she would have already blacked out from it all. She wondered how long she could go. She wondered how long she could last.

"That's right. That's a good girl. Take it. Take all of it for me. Such a good little slut."

The bed was a battering ram hammering against the wall, the mattress bowing beneath their bodies. Tremor after tremor ripped through her, and at last, her wailing cries freed themselves from the barricade behind her tongue. They filled the room, bouncing off of every surface and carrying for seconds, minutes, maybe hours. He fucked her harder, faster, twisting his tongue in her ass and curving his cock in her cunt and dragging her hips up so he had enough space to slap his tail against her clit. She gained control of her hands, reaching up to try and scramble away from him. He yanked her right back onto his cock, picking her up almost completely before using her like a fleshlight and jackhammering into her.

"Ach— !!!"

She was screaming and sobbing, tears streaming freely down her blood red face and nails clawing at the headboard before her into large gouges were left in the wood. She tried to focus on her thoughts, to form some kind of white flag to wave at him before she turned to dust. It felt so good, so fucking good, but she could feel the seams of her being begin to fray, and she knew she had to respect her own limits. She just - didn't want to say his name.

...I can't take anymore. But I don't want you to leave me yet.

The moment the sentiment registered in her mind, his tail relieved her of its stimulation, and his tongue disappeared from her ass. Then the room was shaking, a series of tremors preceding the animalistic roar that left him as he bottomed out inside of her. She emitted a fresh string of shrill cries as he coated her walls, not only from the sensation of his cock violently erupting but also at the feeling of his cum itself. It was more intense than when he had cum all over her. It was both ice cold and white hot, so bizarre that she couldn't focus on any one sensation, and by the time she could even think to, it had dulled to a simple ache, denying her any pain whatsoever.

With another grunt, he slipped out and collapsed in a heap beside her, a rogue chuckle in his wake. She didn't move, focusing on her attempt to gain control of her breathing. Her body felt numb, devoid of energy, and even when she was ready to roll over and finally face him, she simply couldn't. She was once again paralyzed, albeit in a much different way.

Are you - allowed to stay? The thought felt so vague, she was afraid he wouldn't hear it. Then he snorted.

"Of course I'm *allowed* to stay. I just never expected you would want me to."

She furrowed a brow over her heavy eyelids, forcing herself to speak. "Why not?" Her voice was weak and thin, but he heard it all the same.

"You were pretty set on pretending this was all a dream. Conversations tend to make things real."

She gathered the last of her strength, inhaling sharply before she attempted to turn around. However, the weight on the bed beside her suddenly shifted, resettling on the opposite side. When she managed to open her eyes just a sliver, she found him staring at her, his vast form blotting out all else.

"How does - *this* work?"

"Hm. It's - a bit of a complicated system. Are your sure you're coherent enough for it?"

She shrugged. "What happens if I fall asleep here? While I'm already asleep?"

"You'll be much closer to death." Immediately, her eyes snapped wide open. He was grinning. "You won't die though, don't worry. I'd never let that happen."

"So you protect me?"

His face fell slightly. He looked - conflicted. "Not in the traditional sense. I mean I will, and I want to, but - that isn't what I'm supposed to be here for. It's not in my job description, so to speak."

"So what is? Are you like - a nightmare?"

A low chuckle rumbled through him. "Hardly. Nightmares are a thing of *your* making."

"And you're not?"

"I'm what the nightmares run from. Because with or without you, I'm real. I'm eternal."

It was difficult to grasp how ominous the words were when he was looking at her like that, his red eyes softened and his thick fingers tracing the side of her face. How could this ever be real? How could something so abominable look at her with a tenderness that she had rarely ever seen in humans?

Or...maybe that was exactly how. He wasn't human. He could afford it.

"Your soul wanders when you sleep." It took her a moment to register the fact that he was talking. "Not everyone's does, but some people's do."

"Have I done it before?"

"Before you saw me? Maybe, but not so far. I believe that something has yours eager to get away from whatever it is it thinks it's running from." She shut her eyes. "Something happened to you. I can smell it all over you, the fear reserved for something worse than me."

He seemed to be waiting for her to explain, to confirm his suspicions with the truth, but the truth was balled up in her throat, and it refused to be freed. So he kept talking.

"So when a soul wanders, sometimes it crosses a boundary into my realm, which is what yours has done."

"Like - into Hell?"

He chuckled. "Do you believe all demons come from Hell?"

Confusion fluttered across her face. "You don't?"

"Oh, I do." He grinned. She would have to learn his brand of sarcasm, wouldn't she? "Others have different names for it, but this realm is much larger than a singular place. Hell exists here, yes, and it was the first to be built here, but this place encompasses a whole lot more. It's not a place you can reach from Earth either, not without a Reaper."

"A Reaper?"

"Those are your garden-variety demons. The ones you probably know best."

"The ones that possess people?"

"They can. We all *can* really, but it isn't a stipulation of any particular role here. Possession serves a particular purpose, and it's not always a malicious one."

"Like what?"

"Sometimes, demons just need a place to hide."

She wasn't sure what to say to that, but she was fading fast. She focused on the original conversation.

"So what are reapers then?"

"Reapers collect souls. Sometimes before a mortal dies, sometimes after, depending on the situation. And Favors you might know too. Mortals call them crossroads demons."

"You're serious."

"Of course I'm serious. What about my face says otherwise?"

He was still grinning, but she could hardly reprimand him when he turned to face her better and threw an arm over her waist. How she had become so comfortable in his arms —in his mere presence— was beyond her, but after all those nights absent any proper rest, she couldn't find it in herself to complain. Now, she woke up each day well rested. The only problem was that getting out of bed was growing even harder.

She yawned. "You didn't tell me why."

"Why what?"

"Why you want to protect me."

His expression shifted. Not soured, really, but it certainly lost the shine it had sported mere moments ago. His fingers curled against her back, and it was then that she realized the way his antlers curved in on themselves, making it possible for him to lay beside her so comfortably. She wished to touch them, but her arms were made of nothing but lead between them.

"I wish I could tell you, Penelope," he sighed almost sadly.

"I came here for your fear, but like I told you before, once I tasted it, it - it made me ill. I was supposed to stand back and watch, let the nightmares have their fun and feed off the fruits of their labor, but - I couldn't do it. Everything in me rebelled against my one purpose, and it was all for you. So I don't have a reason I can put in a neat little box for you because I don't understand it myself. All I can tell you is that from the first night you saw me and I saw you, my being knows nothing else. It can survive on nothing less than your pleasure. Your peace."

Every word rolled through her like a gentle wave against the shore, carrying away more and more of her apprehension each time. Odd as it was, she had no desire to question this blessing any further.

"It was my father," she squeaked suddenly, but he still pulled her closer to him. He wasn't just warm. He was the perfect temperature. "Six months ago, our - our house was broken into, and - he was staying over. I think they didn't expect him. I'm... When my sister has to go on business trips, I'm usually home alone, but he was there, and-"

"They took him from you, and you could hear it. You could hear him fighting, trying to keep them away from you." She looked up at him, but before she could allow any hope to fester, he shook his head with a grim look of apology. "I can read your thoughts, remember? But don't worry. I couldn't read the ones about your father until you opened them to me. I just didn't want you to have to say it all."

She nodded, deflating but allowing him to pull her fully into his chest. "Do you - is there..."

"Yes, but - what mortals believe in, their Heaven and Hell, it isn't the reality for us and our realm. Sure, those places exist, but it's not so clear cut as those who are bad and those who are good. Those things, when put in the hands of mortals, are very subjective, aren't they? Mortals think they know the difference, but they can only point to the bad or the good when it's someone else being judged."

"So - what does that mean?"

He was quiet for a few minutes, the only sound being the thumping of her heart and the intermittent twitch of his wings. He brushed a hand through her hair. Her eyes fell shut.

"It means your father is fine, Penelope. If he's passed on, it's because he's made peace, and that means you can too."

"I - can you find him? Do you know where he is?"

She didn't mean to sound so desperate, but this felt like an opportunity she couldn't simply turn a cheek to. She had to know. How could she ever find peace if she didn't know.

"Trust me. You don't want me to be able to find him," he assured her. "The Somni Dae, the sleep demons, we don't deal in souls, certainly not those in the pits of Hell, and if he is in Heaven, it's only because that is what he believed in. Is that what he believed in?"

She froze, then shook her head. "We - my father wasn't Christian or anything. I mean, his parents were, and my mother's parents were Hindu, but my parents, they didn't..."

"Look, regardless, there is a place for his beliefs, and wherever that may be, I can assure you he isn't suffering. You have to commit heinous atrocities to end up in The Fires, and if he raised you, I know that isn't true of him. And - besides, Hell is actually a pretty exclusive club, and most of its residents chose to be there. The only ones who are miserable there are those who have done irrevocable harm to people, and - even some of the worst, we've turned away."

"Then where do they go?"

"The only place they deserve to go."

Although she wasn't sure what that place was because before she could ask for further information or he could offer it up, she had begun to sink into this secondary slumber, all too comfortable in his arms. She wanted to ask if he would be there when she awoke, if she could call for him in the event he wasn't, but she was too far gone. She would simply have to wait and see.

8

ACHERON

"You're seriously not gonna share the details? What the fuck is up with that?"

Acheron ignored the collective howls of Idris and the rest of their brethren. The Somni Dae had learned to revel in one another's triumphs, to live vicariously through those few lucky demons who came across a wanderer. And this was different. This was no mere wanderer. It was a wanderer who had consented to touch.

However, Acheron could not relent to this tradition so easily this time because wasn't simply a wanderer who consented to touch either. It was Penelope, and she now possessed claim to the most human parts of him, pieces he never thought existed before. The more he dwelled upon it, the lesser he understood it, but the point was that he was protective of her. To a fault. To the point of ruin.

"He's soft on her," Denek grunted to another round of guffaws. "Look at him."

"You really wanna test how soft I am?" Acheron shot back with a smirk, leaning over the pool table he and Idris had been occupied with for the past half hour. "That isn't it."

"Then what is it? Come on. Why you holdin' out on us?"

"You honestly think you deserve anything from me the way you're actin'?""Only actin' this way because you're holdin' out.""Alright, alright," Idris interrupted, holding up his hands.

The southern pub was strictly the territory of the Somni Dae although they were always eager to welcome other demons into the fold if only for the stories they told. Tonight though, the Reapers were busy with a few mortal mishaps and the Favors had yet to return, so it was only the sleep demons occupying the space. And of course the usual souls who worked and wandered around.

A thick curtain of smoke hung over the room, the sugary sweet scent of herb permeating the air. Card games and pool tables littered the floor alongside endless fountains of mead and marked rum which was made of liquid onyx and fire vines and brewed by the witches who worked with the earth. Unlike mortal alcohol, it could actually get a demon fucked up if he wasn't careful about his consumption, but of course, that was kinda the point.

Music flared amidst all else, much of it mortal and often an acquired taste, but a demon never trekked out to Earth just to come back empty-handed. The Puri especially liked to collect tokens of the innovations they helped influence. Sex, drugs, and party anthems were part of that package. Abyssus didn't reflect the mortal world. The mortal world reflected Abyssus.

"Look, if Acheron wants to hold out, he has every right," Idris went on. "Not to mention, he oversees all of you dick-heads. Maybe if you're good little devils, he'll spare—"

"Acheron!"

The doors of the pub burst open, every creature in the place on high alert and in a defensive position. However, everyone relaxed some when a familiar face appeared framed in the doorway. Greyish red skin and thick horns curled back like a ram. A Reaper.

"Astaroth?"

"Acheron, it's - fuck, it's Xaphan!"

HE DIDN'T REMEMBER what Astaroth said after that. He only remembered running. Or flying or projecting. No, he remembered blinking, and then he was there beside Xaphan, who had been laid across the scorched ground in the center of the city compound. The whispers around him quieted. Someone was summoning Baal. That could only mean one thing.

"They came out of nowhere," someone shouted as the crowd parted around Acheron. "We were right outside the fucking casino, and they attacked."

The casino. That had to mean Mammon's casino, and the only ones who would have attacked so close to a Puri stronghold was the Dominion. Why tonight? Why Xaphan? They had to know that attacking a Son of Lucifer in Sin City was a call to war. Then again, maybe that's why they had done it. Maybe the time had finally come. Maybe Heaven and Hell were about to collide.

Acheron winced as his vision focused on Xaphan's broken body. There was blood everywhere, black and thick and pouring out of multiple gashes in his skin. One of his horns had been broken clean off, and his wings were torn and tattered. It was amazing the left one was still attached to his body. The same could not be said for his right arm up to the elbow.

"Cheron," Xaph chuckled, beckoning him closer with the hand he had left. It hardly left the ground. "I was wondering if you'd come. I know you got a wanderer to tend to."

"What the fuck did you get yourself into, dumbass?"

But Acheron's voice was hoarse. He dropped to his knees beside his oldest friend, reaching for him but unsure where to touch. Xaphan groaned as he reached up and took hold of Acheron's hand.

"The fucking Dominion, would you believe it?" Xaphan went on, still smiling around his bloodstained teeth, some of which were chipped and broken. "They made time for me. That makes me a big fucking deal, don't it, brother?"

"Yeah, a big fuckin' pain in the ass maybe."

"Ah, you always were a jealous bastard, Acheron. It don't suit you."

"Fuck off, Xaph, look at you. Getting fucked up by a White Wing."

"Hey, those little motherfuckers are tougher than they look, and it isn't like they were brave enough to take me one-on-one."

"Did you at least dirty their robes?"

"Oh, you know I did. Took a few limbs too. They'll remember me."

Acheron shook his head. "How did—"

The ground shook around them, and Acheron looked up, watching as the red sky darkened before his eyes. White lightning left multiple fractures in its surface, clouds of ash thickening above. Then, without warning, three vast figures appeared in the square, their forms obscured by cloaks and shadows. The crowd moved back, bowing their heads, and Acheron stood. He knew who they were without further consideration. Of course, he would know his creator anywhere.

Belphegor, Amon, and Leviathan stood before him,

three of the Puri in the flesh. It was not often that Abyssus had the pleasure of welcoming all three at once and in such a public way. Baal came to drink with all of the legions often enough, and Bel and Leviathan checked in with their demons routinely, but they had entire lives on Earth. Like one big Fuck You to the golden gates that glared down at them. Lucifer was nowhere to be found, but he was often nowhere to be found. As for the remaining three, they were no doubt upstairs trying to handle the fall-out. Mammon and Asmodeus were the most terrifying of the seven, and the idea that The Dominion would hang around long enough to run into them was laughable. Acheron sure hoped they did though. It would prove how foolish they had become. And it would make it easier to exact revenge.

It was too late for damage control as far as Acheron was concerned. They came for his brother. And if they came for his brother, they came for him.

The Puri removed their hoods, their horns revealing their identities before their eyes could. Belphegor's mirrored Acheron's, a vast rack of antlers that curved up and in with gold lining the black bone. He gave Acheron a sympathetic nod before kneeling down on the opposite side of Xaphan, assessing the damage. Acheron held his breath. Xaphan was the one constant he had in this existence apart from Belphegor, but there could never be a bond like this one. The Puri knew that. Bel knew that.

Standing again, Belphegor met Acheron's gaze.

"We'll take him to the Helix, see what we can do," he explained. "I'll come find you."

Acheron knew better than to argue. Bel could siphon every ounce of energy and emotion in Acheron's body and sift through it at will, so nothing need be said anyway.

Instead, he simply nodded as Leviathan lifted Xaphan into the air.

Xaphan reached for Acheron's hand, giving it a firm squeeze before letting go.

"Don't mourn me yet, brother," he said with a weak smirk. "I'll be back."

"Yeah, you better. You owe me money, remember?"

"How could I forget?"

As the Puri disappeared into the darkening sky, the crowd began to disperse. Night would fall soon in the waking world, meaning Penelope would be expecting him, but Acheron could hardly move. Something twisted in his gut, anxious nerves clawing at the inner lining of his throat. Had Penny truly softened him so? Not that he would know how his kind normally reacted to losing a close friend. He never had before. He didn't have many, and perhaps this was why. At the very least, this was a lesson. He would hate to have to feel this more than once.

Penelope.

Ignoring further calls of his name from other demons, Acheron headed back to his chambers, following the moon's humble descent. Anger and uncertainty roiled within him, but he swatted them away for the time being, unwilling to look them in the eye. He had no clue how to deal with them, never having had to before. But this was what war looked like. Bel had always said so. Once a war began, everything a demon had ever known would come crashing down, and all the things he had never known would catch up with them. In Acheron's opinion, Asmodeus had given the more pivotal insight.

War will make you every ugly thing the mortals believe you to be, but you'll have to become that if you want to see their world and ours survive.

The only thing he could focus on right now was getting back to Penelope, knowing he could lay his wrath there in her sheets without having to first pick it apart. He could fuck her into a stupor and pretend, for those glorious few hours, that his closest friend wasn't in pieces somewhere. He could look at her and act as though she would last forever.

But that wasn't true. War would come for them too. And if war didn't, reality would. Though he supposed that soon, there wouldn't be much of a difference.

9

PENELOPE

"You look great!"

Jenna's squeals carried across the lawn as she enveloped Penelope in a tight hug, her bags forgotten at her feet. Penelope hadn't even been aware of what day it was until she woke up and saw her sister's text stating she would be home by noon, and by then, it had been half an hour 'til.

"You really have been sleeping, huh?"

"Yes, but not because of those pills," Penelope shot back with a smile, taking a step back.

"Right, yeah, Mama scolded me about it already, thanks."

Penelope shrugged. "I told you I tried them, and I did. And - to be honest, they weren't that bad. I just feel less groggy in the morning with the weed."

"Hey, whatever works. I'm just glad your eyes finally put down the luggage."

Penelope shoved her sister's shoulder, Jenna giggling with unprecedented glee. It was good to see the worry washed from her face after so long with it etched into her skin like a scar. Although now that it was gone, Penelope could at last weigh the sheer volume of it, how it had made Jenna look a decade older most mornings. She knew it had been layered over guilt and grief as well, all of it walled up away from any kind of inquisition that may have befallen her otherwise. She was the eldest. It was what she had been taught to do. Bury her pain so that she may tend to that of others. Penelope never wanted to contribute to that again.

"So Shane stayed over, huh?" Jenna said now, her tone coy.

Penelope rolled her eyes. "Don't start."

"I'm only asking a simple question, Penny."

"Yes, and he's been trying to do it again ever since."

"And what's wrong with that? He's educated, ambitious, handsome. He's practically perfect."

"He's boring."

Penelope had no clue where it had come from. Or rather, she had no clue why she had said it so blatantly, but it was nothing short of the truth. She simply hadn't figured out the word before. Besides, ever since that night, he had become seemingly more eager to come over again. Of course, she was far too preoccupied for that. The only man —or being, she supposed— she wanted around anymore was Acheron, and despite the fact their visits were limited to a specific time and place, she had no will to entertain anyone else. Shane's insistence only enforced that, his advances growing more and more aggressive as the days went by. He wasn't rude or anything. She'd never seen him rude or even mean, but he would ask multiple times a day. At least now, Jenna was home. It was the best possible deterrent to his slumber party offers.

"How is he boring?" Jenna went on, dropping her bags on the couch. "He's smart."

"And yet somehow he manages," Penny sighed. "He's a good friend, and we have a nice time together, but - he's not the type of man I want to come home to every night."

"So what type of man do you want then, Penny?"

The answer was on the tip of her tongue. She didn't want a man at all. She had a demon who waited for her to come back to him each night, and she could not imagine anyone competing with the pleasure Acheron gave her. More than that, no one could ever provide her the safety and security he offered, even if he was worlds away. Even if she could never bring him home to meet her sister.

"At least you know he'd actually come home," Jenna pushed on.

"That's called settling, and you know what Mom says about settling."

They both recited the words. "If we were meant to settle, we would be born with instructions."

Laughter glittered around the kitchen in a way it hadn't in a very long time, and Jenna wrapped an arm around Penelope once more.

"How about we go out for dinner, huh?"the elder offered. "I'll tell you about Toronto then I can break the news about my next trip."

"What? Already? You just got back."

"It's a swift industry, and these conferences are where the money is really. Don't worry though. This one's in the states."

"Oh yeah? What state?"

Jenna shrugged. "Florida."

Penelope rolled her eyes but smiled regardless. "I think I can manage now."

Jenna grinned. "Yeah, I think you can too. Now, come on. My treat."

. . .

After the sisters returned from dinner, Jenna retired upstairs for a hot bath while Penelope finished folding her fresh laundry before preparing for bed. Jenna had informed her that her next trip was only two weeks away, and it would also be another two weeks away from home. Penelope hadn't lied though. She could manage just fine now that she had Acheron although the longer they went on like this, the more she was convinced that there had to be a way for her to see him during the day, to call him to her when she was awake. While she was grateful for the time she was given with him and she knew she didn't need him around all the time, she hated the limitation. And having to medicate every night was troublesome too.

She had tried to fall asleep on her own, but she never stayed asleep, something at the edge of her conscious mind continually pulling her back to the surface. Then there were the nightmares that would creep in, threatening to consume her if she gave them the time of day. She didn't want to waste the night, so she stuck to the weed, allowing herself to relax into real sleep. As she put her laundry away, she eyed her pen on the bedside table with a smile. She glanced at the clock behind it. It was almost time.

She padded out of her room and down the hall to Jenna's, finding her sister combing her hair out on her bed. The TV was on, old reruns playing faintly from it that her sister wasn't really watching.

"I'm going to bed," Penelope informed her, moving to kiss her sister's cheek.

Jenna did the same. "Good night. I'll see you in the morning."

"Yes, you owe me pancakes."

"Whatever you say."

Smiling, Penelope returned to her room, shutting the door before she began to strip down. She didn't bother putting pajamas on anymore, not when Acheron would simply tear them off. Of course, when she awoke, they would still be there, twisted around her body and soaked in sweat. Or, in the case of her panties, her arousal. What was the point?

Getting under the covers, she snatched her pen off of the table and took a long pull, the vapor filling her lungs before she expelled it into the air. The dark felt comforting, a promise of what was to come. She sunk into the sheets with a content sigh, clearing her mind and shutting her eyes. She was pretty good at helping the weed along at this point, and very little could distract her from getting back to him once it was in her system. He was in there too, calling to her, drawing her into the abyss.

The shapes of the shadows beyond her eyelids began to shift, the line between sleep and wakefulness blurring into the black. She felt him before she saw him, before she even opened her eyes. Before she knew she had fallen asleep at all. He filled the room and eclipsed her vision, dampening the harsh reality that would still be there waiting for her when she awoke.

He didn't waste a second. His hands caressed her hips, curling around her thighs until his thumbs could trace the skin up to the apex. As soft as his touch may have been, she could sense his eagerness. It mirrored her own. She squirmed as he spread her open, her body little more than a doll for him to pose but her spirit a wildfire stoked by his every touch. His tongue dipped through the valley of her breasts before encircling each of them, flicking the tip against her nipples until they hardened. He was awakening every part of her in a way she could not explain any further, but she didn't want to. She only wished to feel it.

Though when she opened her eyes at last, she froze. Something was wrong.

He looked - odd, the edges of him errant and out of focus, and his antlers uncurled and chaotic. They looked like a forest of brambles, the kind of thing you could fall into and never find your way out of before you bled out, the tips glinting like blades. And his eyes... His eyes were nearly black beneath those antlers, but the flames behind them were evident. He gripped her hard enough to bruise, his jaw set, not a word spent from his lips.

She gripped his hands before she knew she could, holding them in place. He looked up at her, confusion coloring his expression, but still he said nothing.

"Ach -" She caught herself, using her hold on his hands to sit herself up. He looked away, but she quickly reached for his cheek. She could feel the fury buzzing beneath his skin. And - beneath hers too. Like an aftershock. "Something's wrong."

He shook his large head with a grunt. "Nothing you need to worry about, Penny. Just let me take care of you, huh?"

He reached for her again, but she gripped his face in both her hands, her eyes stern. Where it came from, she wasn't sure, but it was evident to her that he was hurting. She couldn't quite put it into words, but it was almost as though she could feel his emotions coursing through her, kicking up dust and making it hard to breathe. Whatever was wrong, it had to be bad.

"What is it?"

He looked her over the way one would a puzzle, his gaze calculating and unconvinced of where this might end up. She pushed herself up onto her knees. Then she straddled him, keeping his gaze as she waited. There was the flicker, the faintest hint in his eyes that she was right, and terror whipped around her like a chill wind.

"My -" He started slowly, his mouth forming around each of the words like a mold. "My oldest friend was attacked tonight."

"What? Is - are they okay?"

Acheron shrugged, releasing a deprecating laugh. "I don't know. He was nearly in fucking pieces when I saw him, and I - I don't know."

"Well - where is he? If you need to go to him, you can—"

He shook his head, cupping one of the hands on his cheek with his own. "The Puri, our - creators, they have him. They're trying to fix him, but wounds like that from - from Dominion blades, they can't always be healed."

There was so much he wasn't saying, and she could feel it whirling within her too, a storm that could not be contained nor compressed down into a few neat sentences. She realized then just how big the world truly was, how he wasn't simply confined to this layer of her room and he lived an entire life outside of her. Demons lived entire lives outside of humans, and it was infuriating how naive she'd been this whole time. How self-centered. And all because she had wanted to pretend he wasn't real.

"We have to be careful now," he went on with a deep breath. "The Dominion, they don't seem to be playing by the rules anymore. Or they're making new ones, and I know mortals are taught that when it comes to angels and demons, it's good vs. evil, but - it's not that simple. It's never that simple."

"So - are you in danger?"

He chuckled again, but she could see him begin to shrink as if this burden was weighing him down and pressing him straight into the ground right before her eyes.

"We're all in danger, Penelope." He took hold of her chin now. "If they start changing the rules for us, they will start changing the rules for you. And if they get rid of us, champions of your mortal free will, what will you have left but chains?"

If Penelope was being honest, she didn't care much about anything at the moment but him, the mere insinuation that she could lose him so soon making her skin crawl. Of course he could read that from her thoughts if not right off of her face, and he shook his head slowly.

"You don't have to worry about me, Penny," he assured her. "It will take a bit more than this to keep me away from you."

"I don't want you to get hurt."

"I'm much safer than Xaphan was. He's a reaper, and they caught him while he was out in the waking world. I never leave my realm, and they don't come down here. At least not yet. It'll be awhile before then, but - we just have to be prepared." He licked his lips, brushing his thumb along her lower one. "I shouldn't have told you. I don't need you worryin' about things you can't change."

"I mean, I asked. I wanted to know. I could - I can feel it. Your pain."

He smirked, looking down between them. "Then it seems like you're not the only one who left a mark."

"I guess not." She leaned forward, resting her forehead against his.

"And to think you believed I wasn't real."

Penelope shut her eyes. "You're the realest thing in my life right now."

"And I'm not going anywhere."

He wrapped his arms around her, and she sunk deeper into his warmth, allowing herself to be comforted by the simple sentiment. She couldn't say she completely understood what it was he was saying to her. War seemed like such an ambitious idea. More than that, it was difficult to envision such an overarching storyline. It was one thing to know she was a single person among billions on a single planet in a single galaxy, but to now expand the existing world beyond realms and dimensions? How did one make peace with that?

She decided it was not important at the moment. No, what was important was that her words were true. He was more real than anything else to her, and he offered the only comfort she had known since the death of her father. Whether it was truly a dream or not, she refused to consider an alternative. More specifically, she refused to consider the alternative of living without him.

Pulling back, she pressed her mouth to his. It was the first time they'd kissed, her tongue sliding between his lips and her hands grasping his neck. She'd forgotten she was bare until her nipples rubbed up against the coarse skin of his chest, a moan escaping her at the sensation. One of his hands moved down her body at a sluggish pace, stimulating each inch of skin he came into contact with.

"Promise me you'll always come back to me," she whimpered the moment their lips parted.

His eyes met hers. "I swear to you, Penelope, I will always come back to you."

10

PENELOPE

"So you're really sleeping? That's wonderful, Penelope!"

Belinda's voice was heavy with genuine excitement, and Penelope could feel her therapist smiling through the phone. She smiled too. It felt good to finally give that update. She knew she wasn't completely healed. She also knew no one expected her to be. But the fact that she was making such drastic progress meant a lot to her even if it came with a few questionable habits. Like fucking a demon and sleeping in to do so. Of course, she'd left those parts out.

"Yes, and I'm only on the weed now," Penelope stated proudly. "I don't even need the pills."

"And how do you feel? It's one thing to sleep but to feel rested..."

"I feel great actually."

She stared at her reflection in her vanity mirror. Much of the color had returned to her face, her brown eyes blooming with a crisp kind of gleam she hadn't seen in months. Her hair looked healthy, and she felt light, almost unburdened by anything in the physical world. Even getting out of bed was growing easier, which was difficult to imagine when it was going to sleep that made her most content. The irony of that alone made her giddy because just weeks ago, the mere thought of going to sleep drove her headfirst into a panic. Oh, how times could change.

"So your sister is leaving on another trip, right?" Belinda went on. "When is that?"

"Day after tomorrow."

"And how do you feel about it?"

"Better than I did about her last one. I feel confident that I can get through it."

"Which is definitely an improvement from where we were even a month ago. I'm really proud of you, Penny. You have no idea."

"Thank you, Linda, I appreciate that."

"And while you sleep, do you dream at all?"

Penny smiled to herself. "Not really. Nothing I can remember at least."

"We will take it then, but just in case, how about you start keeping a dream diary for me? It doesn't have to be excessive. It could just be a note in your phone, but it will give us a new place to start outside of the night terrors."

"O-okay, yeah, sure. I can do that."

"Great. Talk next week, same time?"

"Sounds good."

After ending the call, Penelope pocketed her phone and headed downstairs into the kitchen. It was her night to cook dinner, and she and Jenna had done their bi-weekly grocery shopping earlier in the day so that she could grab the necessary ingredients. It was the first time in a long time she was able to put some effort into her recipe. Usually she either just shelled out for takeout or settled for making something easy like tacos. However, today had arguably been the best day she'd had since the incident in terms of attention and energy. She refused to waste it.

Penelope hummed to herself as she arranged several chicken breasts and various additional ingredients into a Pyrex dish before shoving it all in the oven. She then got started on the salad, chopping up olives and tomatoes and tossing them into a bowl of vivid green lettuce and spinach. As she looked through their available dressings, the doorbell rang.

"I got it!" Jenna yelled from the living room.

The security system beeped three times, signaling that an exterior door had been opened, followed by the low murmur of a conversation Penny couldn't make out. A few minutes passed before she heard footsteps approaching the kitchen. She glanced over her shoulder just as Jenna appeared in the archway.

"Look what the wind swept in," she announced in a singsong voice.

Shane appeared behind her with a sheepish smile on his face, giving Penny a short wave. Penny swallowed, her gut twisting suddenly in a disorienting way. She couldn't be certain what it meant, but it eventually morphed into a distinct annoyance, an insistent discomfort rooted in the fact that he was now simply showing up at her home after she had turned down his offers to stop by and hang out on multiple occasions. All she could manage was a small smile before she looked to her sister, who seemed to gather quite quickly that she'd made a mistake.

"I asked Shane if he wanted to stay for dinner," she explained, her gaze apologetic before turning to him. "But you gotta be out after that because it's Sister Sister Movie Night, and that can't be trespassed upon."

"I can abide by that," he agreed after a momentary pause.

"Good. Now make yourself at home in the living room, and I'll get you a beer."

Shane didn't think to linger, disappearing back through the doorway while Jenna sidled up to her sister with a pointed look.

"There is something you left out the other night when I asked about him, isn't there?"

Penelope stared at her, eyes wide. "I - I don't know. I mean no, not then, but I - can we talk about it after dinner?"

"Oh, you better believe we can."

Jenna kissed her cheek before stalking towards the fridge to dig out a beer. With a sigh, Penelope opened the oven to check on the chicken before beginning to mash the potatoes she had boiled earlier. As she buttered and salted them, she tried to control her nerves as well.

While much of her irritation could be attributed to the fact that she wanted nothing to do with anyone but Acheron at the moment —Jenna being the exception—, that didn't negate the fact that she had been clear with him dozens of times. Regardless of her reasons, she didn't want nor need the company. And she didn't feel she owed him any additional qualifications for peace.

She'd never felt unsafe around him before, but at the moment, she felt uneasy, and she didn't like that at all. But she could be civil because he was her friend, and he did always try and look out for her, especially after her father was killed. She decided the best thing to do was to get through the night as quickly and quietly as possible, and once she discussed it with Jenna, maybe it would be easier to maintain that distance for however long it took for her to get over these emotions.

Once dinner was ready, she called everyone to the table where she'd already set out food, plates, and utensils. Shane and Jenna were discussing some new software Jenna's firm had just finished developing, Shane offering some ideas for security. Penny poured herself and Jenna each a glass of wine and handed Shane another beer before she took a seat beside her sister.

"So you must have a lot of freedom in your schedule if you're working independently most of the time, right?" Jenna asked as she slapped mashed potatoes on her plate, more than happy to maintain control of the conversation. "Or are you also obligated to attend a dozen conferences a year?"

"Oh, we have a few here and there, but definitely not as frequently as you," he replied. "But yeah, I arrange my own schedule usually unless there's some major project going on. I spend most of my time fixing patches and stuff, a lot less time developing anything new, but there is definitely a decent amount of freedom. It'll be a huge help when I get back into classes."

"Are you still going for psychology, or are you committing to this cyber nerd thing?"

He rolled his eyes with a grin. "Look who's talking!"

"Oh, I never denied it. It wasn't meant to be an insult."

"You know, I actually haven't decided yet. When I signed on for the cyber security certification, it seemed like a short term fix to the long term problem, but now? This gig has done me a whole lot of good, and I think I could climb the ranks just as well with nothing more than experience at this point, but additional training wouldn't hurt."

"Yeah, I hear those certification classes can be pretty pricey too. It would be a shame to just let it go."

"Well, with the money I-"

He looked up suddenly, frozen in his seat, his eyes wide. The sudden silence seized the unwavering attention of both sisters, and they looked up at him with scrutinizing gazes. It felt as though he had only just caught himself from saying something he hadn't meant to, and Penelope found herself curious as to what it might have been.

Yet all he said was, "Well it was leftover money from my loans really." He chuckled, another bashful smile on his reddened face, and Penny wasn't sure she believed him. "I just scraped by long enough to land this job, which I owe more to one of my fraternity brothers than anything. He really talked me up."

"You always seemed so committed to the psychology track though," Penny said now although she was unsure why. "What changed?"

He shrugged, a heavy sigh leaving him. "Don't get me wrong. It still interests me, but the world is changing. And what's morally good isn't always financially sound anymore."

He ducked his head then, cramming a forkful of mashed potatoes into his mouth. Penelope watched him carefully. Maybe she was just overly agitated with him and now everything he did rubbed her wrong, but something about that sentence, about his tone when he said it, made her feel uneasy. Glancing at Jenna, it was evident that she felt the same, confusion and discomfort coloring her eyes. No one said anything for a long time after, and once they finished eating, Penelope quickly began cleaning up so as to signal to him that they were nearing the end of his visit. Jenna busied herself with setting up the living room for the girls night they were now apparently going to have, no longer eager — or able— to fake a smile on his behalf. Penelope hated having to lie just to protect his pride, but something was nagging at her, something that told her it was best to continue the charade until he was out of the house. To keep the peace.

"You're not mad at me for showing up, are you?"

His sudden appearance beside her at the sink made Penelope nearly jump out of her skin, but she managed to suppress the gasp or scream that threatened to leave her. She did fumble a fork, but she simply grabbed a plate and continued washing.

"Huh? Oh, no, I just-"

She shrugged, wondering what would be worse: Telling him the truth and risking an argument or not telling the truth and being blamed later for not being honest. She kept her eyes on the water running into the sink, placing the plate on the dish rack and pouring more liquid soap onto her dish wand. With a slow breath, she pushed herself forward.

"I told you I was alright, that I just needed some time for myself," she said softly.

"I know, but I've been worried about you. You know all I've wanted is to be there for you, right? To - to support you after—"

"And I get that, but sometimes supporting me means giving me my space and letting me figure things out for myself. I can't lean on everyone else forever."

"You can always lean on me, Penny."

She looked over at him at last and again had to bite her tongue. There was nothing overtly insidious about his face, but - there were shadows cast across it, shadows she wasn't sure the lighting in the kitchen could possibly create. There was also something about his eyes that made her want to shrink in on herself. She was suddenly acutely aware of the fact that she was about to be in this house alone for the next two weeks, but even if she hadn't been, he would've reminded her mere moments later.

"Jenna will be gone for another couple weeks, right?"

Jenna must have told him when she first opened the door because Penelope had been vigilant about what was uttered during dinner, and she certainly hadn't said a word to him about it prior.

"Yeah, but I'll probably go down and see my mom," she said quickly but not too quickly, placing a plate in the dish rack.

"Well, I could bring you by some weed before you go, make sure you—"

"I can stop at a dispo on the way. Plus, I've been having it delivered by a place nearby, so I can get some there if need be. No worries."

"Penny, is—"

"Hey!" Jenna poked her head into the kitchen. "Do those later. I've already got the movie ready. And you, sir." She pointed at Shane with a wink. "You have to go, but it was super fun having you for dinner."

"Uh, yeah, we should do it again when you get back," he managed, obviously not expecting them to actually kick him out. "I'll even cook next time."

"That is definitely on the table."

Jenna's quick look at her sister assured Penelope it was not.

He turned back to Penelope for a brief moment, who was taking her time washing her hands. He leaned over and kissed her cheek. She clenched her jaw.

"I'll text you later," he whispered. "Call me if you need anything at all, alright?"

"Thank you," she managed.

She didn't watch as he retreated, fixated on her

breathing and the insistent thud of her heart. She heard the system beep when the front door opened then a few moments of chattering voices before the door closed again. Another long beep alerted her to the fact that Jenna had armed the system, and then seconds later, her sister was standing in the kitchen at her shoulder. Penny turned to her, towel in her hands and terror in her veins. They stared at one another for the longest time, tension taut in the air. Then Jenna shattered the silence.

"What the fuck?"

All Penelope could do was shake her head, the faintest shrug of her shoulders accompanying the motion. It was only now that he was gone that she could truly process the sheer capacity of her nervous energy. She shuddered under the memory of the kiss to her cheek, the skin there now feeling as though it was burning.

"What happened, Penny?"

Penny shrugged again, tossing the towel on the counter. "I - I don't know. I don't know how to explain it. It's just - ever since that night he stayed, he's been trying to push me into another sleepover or something, and I've been adamant about needing space, but he just... It's not that he was - threatening or anything."

"I sure fucking hope not."

"It just feels like - like he has some kind of ulterior motive, you know? And I know he likes me, but it feels like more than that. Like that doesn't even matter anymore. — And what was that at dinner?"

"Right!" Jenna gestured wildly with her hands. "Who says something like that? Especially knowing about Dad, like - yeah, that's what the assholes who broke into our house believed too."

It clicked then. It clicked, and Penelope was almost ill

with the thought. It kicked her in the stomach and pried apart her ribcage before constricting around her heart. *No.*

She quickly straightened, exhaling a heavy breath.

"I don't know, he's just - being pushy," she went on, trying to close the conversation. "I get he's trying to help, but he doesn't get that he isn't. He can't. It's fine though."

"I don't want him showing up here and surprising you while I'm gone."

"I told him I was gonna go stay at Mom's."

"And maybe that's not such a bad idea."

Penelope chewed her lip. "No, maybe not."

Jenna only stared at her, but she pushed the subject no further, instead allowing Penelope to insist they follow through on this movie night and forget all about Shane. And Penelope truly wished she could do it too, forget about him, pretend he didn't exist, but that wasn't an option, was it? Certainly not now. She supposed she would have to find another.

11

ACHERON

The Helix, fortunately, was not a place Acheron often visited, but its architecture had always fascinated him. Its jet black walls twisted and spiraled high up into the air, disappearing into the ash and blood and painted the sky. It was the only structure that penetrated every level of Hell, and it was also the most necessary. It was the one place where the witches could enter Hell, and it was also the one place in Hell where their powers would work without special permission from the Puri. And they needed to work. This was where the infirmary was located.

The halls of the Helix were an intricate maze, easy to get lost in and difficult to escape, especially for those who were held under a disorientation spell in order to receive proper and prolonged care. Some of the halls were illuminated by white lights and wailing screams while others were bathed in blood red lanterns and hallowed silence. Despite his rare visits, Acheron knew exactly where to go, and he headed down one of the halls that mirrored the latter, heading for the Reapers' dedicated wing.

He had found out the day after he last saw Xaphan that

his friend wasn't the only one attacked that night. Other Reapers had been confronted too, three of which never stood a chance. They were younger demons with limited power, erased from this world with one quick cut of a blade. Acheron flexed his fingers before balling up his fists. The wrath remained there, stagnant in his gut, waiting for an outlet.

Xaphan was sitting up in his bed, smoke curling from his lips, when Acheron entered his room. The Reaper smiled, placing his joint in the ashtray on his bedside table before gesturing Acheron closer. The two hugged, Xaphan throwing his good arm around Acheron's waist and Acheron cradling him around the shoulders. They let the silence linger for a time, the red walls surrounding his four-poster bed holding their breath in wait. When the two parted, Acheron sat on the edge of the bed beside Xaphan's legs, looking over his friend with concern in his eyes.

"I'm doing much better than I look," Xaphan assured him although Acheron could see the remnants of fear all over his face. "My healer says the leg will take some time to grow back, and my wings will need a good amount of rest, but it could be worse, right?" He looked up at the ceiling. Or through it. "It was for my charges."

"What the fuck happened, Xaph?" Acheron breathed out.

Xaphan dropped his head then, and it was almost as though whatever was binding him together suddenly came loose. The pain, the anguish, the anger, it all came seeping out of him to settle between the two of them. Acheron wished he could pick it all up and swallow it whole or feed it to the creatures of the wood. Yet all he could do was wait for a response.

"It wasn't anything fantastical, I can tell you that,"

Xaph sighed. "We only had three souls to collect that night, one of which had been promised to me years ago, one I'd been looking forward to, right? No toes out of line, no steps in the wrong direction, no side quests or anything. We show up, I meet the mortal, she's already made peace with her fate. It's done, and we get ready to come home. Then we hear about this whole ordeal at the casino, mortals gambling with their souls and then trying to back out when the chips are already down. Literally. You know Mammon likes chaos, but chaos is bad for business right now, so Baal sends us over to help straighten it out quick. The whole fucking thing must've been a setup because as soon as we get there, I know something's wrong. We don't even make it inside, Acheron. The next thing I know, we're being surrounded by fucking Seraphim, and all I can do is yell, tell the others to go back, to get Mammon or—"

He trailed off, his face distorted and disorienting. He held his hands out, the one that had been missing before slowly growing back but currently no more than a bulb at the end of his forearm, and shook his head. Acheron had never seen him lose his composure. He had seen him angry, frustrated, disappointed, but even then, he had never seen him like this. Speechless. Lost.

"It was Rafael who got me."

"What?"

Acheron's brows furrowed, his wings twitching. *Rafael.* The name always garnered a visceral reaction from every demon. He was one of the three heads of the Dominion as well as the most vicious, but as far as Acheron knew, he never left the safety and comfort of his realm.

"He wanted me to give the Puri a message," Xaphan went on, his voice thick with grief. "He wanted them to know the game had changed, that it's open season now, and we are no longer welcome on Earth."

"How can they do that? They can't do that."

"They seem to think they can."

They couldn't. The Puri had been established on Earth for millenia, long after Asmodeus had infiltrated The Dominion's beloved garden, and they adhered to the code they had set for themselves ages ago. Time and time again, The Dominion had tried to intervene, to push them back down into Hell, and time and time again, their efforts had been thwarted with uncanny ease. So what was different? What had changed?

"And what did the Puri say?" Acheron asked quietly.

"They weren't happy, but they also weren't about to tell me their plan. I - the look in their eyes though. They aren't going to take that laying down. You know that as well as I do, and when the time comes, you know what has to happen."

"A war."

"A war."

Another wave of rage collided with a dousing of white hot shame within Acheron's bones. *War*. How could a word so small encompass an influence so vast. It was not simply a syllable. It was a hungry void, a gluttonous abyss, waiting to devour all who would participate, even those so willing to feed it in the first place. The mortals thought they understood war, but they were mere children playing with toys and toying with lives. They did not understand what it meant to go to war. They fought for different flavors of the same beliefs, for liars and peddlers of political propaganda, for the unchecked attempts at absolute power. They screamed about good vs. evil but had never seen such a battle. And they never would. Because nothing so clear cut had ever existed. Nothing so clear cut ever could.

If this war occurred, it would not be for good or for evil. It would only be for the belief that one held about the other. It would cost one of them everything. And if Acheron and his brethren lost? It would cost *everyone* everything.

But the mortals didn't know that, and if they turned on The Puri before this was over, all would be lost.

"When you're with her, your wanderer," Xaphan began cautiously, bringing Acheron back to the room. "You be careful, brother. You be careful, and you watch yourself because they no longer care about the rules or the guidelines. Something's happening up there. Maybe the big guy is just fed up with playing the part, but either way, the world isn't what it was a week ago much less a few months ago. I need you to understand that. Do you?"

Acheron nodded firmly. "I do, and I promise you. I'll be careful."

"And-" He scratched his chin. "She'll need to be careful too. If they find out you have any attachment in the waking world, they will take it from you, and once they do that, they will find a way to use it against you. They aren't gatekeepers anymore, Acheron. Rafael and his angels, they're hunters, and they're out for all of us. They will do anything they have to do in order to tear us up from the root."

Maybe Acheron did not yet grasp the full meaning of war either, but looking into Xaphan's eyes, he could understand what was at stake. Penelope. And if Penelope was at stake, there would certainly be a war waged because he had promised her, and even then if he hadn't, there was no other alternative. It would take all of Heaven to keep him from her, and even then, well... He would love to see them try.

. . .

After leaving the Helix, Acheron stopped to check in with the other sleep demons. It was evident that everyone was on edge after the attack on the Reapers, but many were oblivious to the details, and that kept mass panic at bay. Something so - *mortal* had never touched down in Hell that way, and Acheron hoped they could stave it off for the time being.

He only stayed at the Somni Dae's pub for an hour or two before returning to his chambers, lying in wait for Penelope's arrival. By now, he could set a watch by her, and he was smitten by the fact. He was smitten by everything about her really, but he was taking the acceptance of that reality at a gradual pace.

Yet... as her world descended upon his own, excitement turned to suspicion turned to consternation. Something wasn't right. The room, it was off. The temperature plummeted. The shadows deepened, darkened. Vines of sharp leaves crept up the walls. Roots fractured the paint, spreading along the baseboards, and carpet and soil overlapped one another until it was impossible to tell who was invading who.

A clock was ticking somewhere, a bell tinkling at the top of each minute. Several rang out before Penelope materialized on the bed, tucked beneath the sheets so tightly that it would have been impossible for her to move whether she was paralyzed or not. Her face was contorted in a mixture of fear and panic. Her eyes were screwed shut. Acheron watched from the foot of the bed, her emotions sinking into him like teeth.

What the hell is happening?

Was it a trap? Had the Dominion found her already, prepared to use her as a gateway into the realm? No, that couldn't be it. They wouldn't be that foolish, that reckless.

They had no power in Hell, and even if they did, it would never be enough to take all of its legions.

Then Penelope started screaming.

Acheron stiffened, curling into the shadows and obscuring his presence. He scanned the room, which seemed so much larger now, searching for the perpetrator who had dared try and bring harm to him through her. But... it was no angel that appeared in the corner opposite him.

The hulking figure stepped out of the darkness, its outline smudged as if it were made out of smoke and its features almost indiscernible because of it. Even so, there was something almost familiar about the form, but Acheron could not even begin to guess why. It resembled a mortal, but the only mortal here was Penelope. She was the only mortal who could be here. Unless...

Wait.

The figure was beginning to clear, but its skin remained washed out and desaturated, leaving the eyes sunken deep into the sockets and the mouth slack. Its edges remained distorted, but as it closed in on the bed, it continued to grow, not just in size but in volume. It looked more solid than it had at first, and it cast a large shadow across the room. Penelope screamed louder. Acheron gritted his teeth. It wasn't a mortal. It was a night terror. And it had followed her all the way down here.

He didn't think twice about it. Acheron cut out of the corner, his claws drawn and his teeth bared. The night terror didn't seem to notice him, but he didn't care. He tore straight through it, burying his claws into its chest and yanking upward towards its head with all his strength. The tear of flesh echoed through the space, followed by the feigned gurgling of a false mortal. Thick black blood oozed down Acheron's arm, plagued with the stench of death and rot.

Penelope was still screaming.

He dropped his arm, letting the body fall to the ground where the earth claimed it. The smell began to fade. The carpet thickened. The grass faded. When he turned around, she was sitting up in the bed, staring at him. The screaming died down once she realized who he was, but the terror in her eyes remained. Then she was up, standing atop the mattress and rushing towards him. He caught her at the edge of the bed, hugging her tight to his chest as he breathed out a sigh of relief.

"Penny, what—"

Yet before he could ask one of the many questions he had regarding the oddity of a night terror's presence here, she was crushing her mouth against his with bruising passion. He could hardly deny her either, regardless of his concerns, instead giving himself over to her whims. Because he had his own troubles he wanted to escape, and this kiss seemed to fill a void he wasn't aware existed somewhere deep inside him. He chased that feeling as long as he could too, the feeling of being whole, cramming it into his mouth like the shameless glutton he was.

Pulling back, she relieved herself of her nightgown, which he had only just noticed she was wearing. It had been a long while since she'd come dressed, but he wasn't complaining. Watching how eager she was to get it off had him salivating, a deep growl rumbling in his chest. Immediately, he ducked his head, nipping at her breasts and leaving angry lines when he scraped his teeth along the swell of them. Her hands curled around his antlers, which curled in on themselves, the points dulling. She pulled him closer. He took hold of a nipple before sucking her breast fully into his mouth.

"Ah!"

Her moans grew in volume as his movements grew in intensity, his hands gripping her ass hard enough to bruise and his mouth greedy against her tits. She ground into him, wrapping one arm around his neck, her mouth pressed against his forehead.

"Needy girl," he grumbled, smacking her ass and earning a yelp. "Are you ever sated?"

"Not with you," she confessed, her voice eager as she continued to rut against his stomach, her bare pussy leaving a trail of arousal down his abdomen.

"You don't wanna play the game tonight, hm?"

She shook her head. "No. I just want you to fuck me. I want you to fuck me until I can't take anymore, and I want you to know how much I enjoy it."

He grinned. "Gladly."

Laying her down on the bed, he kept his eyes locked on hers as his tongue unraveled, disappearing between them so that he could curl it against her clit. She gasped, her back arching and her eyelids fluttering. He reached down, taking hold of his quickly hardening cock and giving it a few rough tugs. It was only then that he realized the depth of his yearning, a festering wound in the pit of his belly that needed immediate attention. He could not wait any longer.

Slotting their hips together, he sunk into her heat with a snarl, her hands on his hips and her teeth in her lip. She whimpered with every inch he bestowed upon her, buried inside her, and he pressed down harder on her clit with the tip of his tongue. He watched every expression, devoured every reaction, feeding off of the sheer ecstasy in her eyes.

That's a good girl. His own voice echoed back at him from

within her thoughts. *You take this cock so well. But you're my greedy little slut, aren't you? Always eager. Always willing.*

"Yes!" She shouted the response at the top of her lungs. "Yes, I am."

"What? What are you?"

"Y-yours! I'm you're greedy little slut. I'm yours. I - ah!"

He slammed into her hard and fast, taking hold of her hands and pinning them above her head with one of his own. The other rested around her neck with the lightest pressure, his thumb running over her lips until she parted them and took hold of it, laving his skin with her own tongue. The motion was soon interrupted by another harsh cry, her eyes rolling back in her head. His cock expanded within her, the ridges all but imprinting on her walls each time she constricted around him. She attempted to hook her legs around his waist, but they slipped down until her heels rested on the backs of his thighs, her body and the bed rocking in time with his hips.

"You think you can stand to take a bit more, Needy girl? Do you think you can handle it?"

She nodded blindly, her wrists limp in his hand, but her pleas reverberated between them, filling his mind and driving his stroke like a candle lit beneath him. Thrust after merciless thrust was accompanied only by strangled cries and labored roars as he squeezed her slim throat in his massive hand, his tongue circling her clit before pressing down on it every now and again.

"Ach—"

She went rigid, her body convulsing beneath him to the point that he pulled his tongue off of her completely although he didn't stop fucking her. He could hear her sputtering out every syllable of his name again and again, broken up by wayward strings of butchered obscenities. He leaned down, dragging his tongue up from her belly to the dip between her breasts to the column of her throat where his hand had just vacated from. That hand was now beneath her thigh, pushing it upward and out in order to stretch her impossibly further. While she couldn't be harmed here, she was conscious enough in his realm to feel both pleasure and pain, and so he was careful to read her body in order to ensure he didn't cause her even the slightest discomfort beyond what was necessary. She wasn't complaining though of course.

"Don't - stop," she breathed, her eyes half lidded and her breathing heavy. "Don't. Please"

"Ah, we really are greedy tonight, aren't we?"

"Y-yes. Yes, please. More."

He obliged without further inquiry. It was as impossible to deny her as it was to deny himself, and there was no reason to try. Her hands remained idle above her head once he released them, instead taking hold of both of her ankles and opening her up impossibly further. He allowed his tail to slip beneath her, probing her ass while his tongue tickled her clit once more. He watched her lick her lips before biting down on the lower, her eyes shut in unadulterated bliss. That image alone had him glowing with pride.

She came undone again gradually and then all at once, her body enveloped by one dramatic shudder as she soaked the sheets and clamped down on his shaft. Even then, she kept drawing him into her with her trembling legs, a vague plea for more clawing its way out of her mouth. Nothing had ever been more rewarding, more fulfilling than her pleasure, and once he took a moment to savor that, it nearly knocked him over.

His head fell back, his hands descending her legs to grasp her thighs as he bottomed out repeatedly. He leaned forward until her knees were damn near touching her breasts, her hands at last coming up to grip his antlers again, to keep him close while he folded her in half. He placed one knee on the bed beside her, then the other, the bed shrieking in protest beneath the weight of his cock jackhammering into her cunt.

"Please! Please!"

What she was begging for, neither of them knew, but it did not matter. He only had one thing on his mind, and that was to get off on the way she begged.

His orgasm crept right up on him, crashing through his frame like a freight train and eclipsing his vision with bright, white light. He coated her walls in his seed, and her cunt spit it all back at him, leaving his abdomen slick as their mixed arousal spilled out onto the sheets below. Both their cries of pleasure and shudders of satisfactions were synced up, complementing one another as they each broke apart. All else melted away, leaving him both lighter and heavier all at once. The latter won out.

Still holding his antlers, she guiding his head down to rest against her neck as he collapsed atop her. Her breathing slowed beneath his weight, but she didn't complain, her hands roaming his back and sides with gentle touches. They remained that way for several seconds or minutes or hours before he carefully maneuvered them further onto the bed and away from the edge. Turning over, he cradled her against him, his arm around her waist and half her body draped over his own. She rested her head on his chest, and he could feel her heart hammering against his ribs. He combed his fingers through her hair, listening to her breathing as he came down from his high.

It was then that he remembered how tonight had begun.

It was obvious that her thoughts were doing everything

in their power to avoid the memory, but it was there, standing at the back like a lone stranger trying to remain undetected. He considered whether or not to ask, but when the memory began to grow, he knew it was no small matter. And that hadn't just been a random night terror.

"Who was he?" he asked, his tone cautious.

There was no immediate response, but the soft sigh she expelled against his chest assured him she had heard the question. He was patient, allowing her to walk into the conversation at her own pace. Though before she could work up the nerve to answer, the vague details of the night terror's features clicked into place for him. He hummed. There was something familiar about the face he was envisioning, but he could not pinpoint the memory. He must have shared his curiosity though because she nodded.

"Shane." Her voice was hoarse. "The man who was staying in my house the first night you and I..."

He tensed. "Did he do something to you?"

"No, I - well, I don't know actually."

He glanced down at her, hardly containing his growing rage. "What do you mean, Penelope?"

"I—"

She paused again, and he could feel her mounting frustration. Pushing herself up so that she could look at him properly, she gave him a worried look. He sat up against the headboard as well, drawing her into his lap.

"He's -" She continued to struggle, pinching the bridge of her nose. "I've been asking him for space, time to - to get used to being on my own. And admittedly, it was an excuse to spend my time with you, but I can't exactly say that, so I just said I needed space, but - he kept pushing it and pushing it, and tonight, he showed up out of nowhere, and my sister invited him to stay for dinner because she didn't know. But - I don't know, he made us both uncomfortable at dinner. He was acting kind of strange, but - what got to me was - there was something he said, something that sounded so familiar."

"What was it?"

"He said - 'what's morally good isn't always financially sound anymore', and I don't know if maybe I'm just - mixing up memories or if I'm paranoid or—"

She searched frantically for the words, but her thoughts laid it out more clearly than words ever could.

"Do you trust me?"

She gave him a questioning look. "After all the things I've let you do to me? What do *you* think?"

He rolled his eyes, his lips twitching, before he reached up to cradle her head in his hand. She relaxed into his palm, moving closer.

"Close your eyes," he whispered.

She hesitated for only a second before obeying him, and he did the same. Focusing his energy, he stepped inside her mind, entering further than he usually would. Searching out her memories with great care, it took him some time to navigate to them, but once he managed to unearth them, they were easy to sort through. He scanned image after image and clip after clip, attempting to match the words she'd uttered to one of them, any of them. The images began to change from vivid and vibrant to worn and grey, the framing growing older while Penelope grew younger. Then, at last, he came across one that echoed the sentiment if not the phrase word for word.

While most of Penny's memories were neatly filed in chronological order, there had been some exceptions, and this one seemed to have been buried beneath all else. Yet its veins were welded into the walls of her subconscious, creeping across the forefront like vines just beneath the surface. He knew what it was before he fully inspected it. It was from six months ago, and even from the pit she had buried it in, it haunted her.

In this country, being morally good will never be as important as being financially good.

Penelope gasped.

Acheron opened his eyes to find her staring back at him, her eyes blown wide and her lips parted in shock. The dialogue of her memory bounced back at him, a boomerang that cut him just as deep if only so that her emotions could infiltrate his very being through the wound. Somehow, he understood.

"I forgot," she breathed, her eyes glazed over. "I forgot he spoke to me."

"If you think he had something to do with it, Penelope, we can find out." He spoke slow and low as if afraid he might spook her. "I can go in and try and clear it up, but you have to remember. You have to—"

She was already shaking her head. "I can't, 'Cheron, I can't. I - I'm not ready."

He didn't miss the shortening of his name, the trust that underlined it, the safety it imbibed. He would smile if this weren't so sensitive.

"Okay, but - I can't let him get away with it if he did this, Penelope."

"Who would ever believe me? Who would ever listen? They caught his friends, and none of them talked. I told them there were four guys. I told them. I was sure of it, and they tried to say I was disoriented, that I was under duress, and that's true, but I wasn't wrong. I wasn't! The man who was in my room got away! He got away, and they didn't even try! So why would they believe me?"

"Hey." He took her face in his hands, his voice stern. "I never said anything about your useless cops. I can take care of it, but you have to trust me completely. Can you do that?"

She stared at him for what felt like ages, worrying her lip until it bled. He ran his thumb over it. She nodded.

"It won't be easy. It won't be comfortable. It may even be worse than remembering, but I promise you that once it's done, if you want me to wipe this memory or any other, I will do it."

Her brows knitted together. "You can do that?"

He nodded although a grimace crossed his face. It was no easy task, and it came at a high cost to him. Hell, every step in this plan coming together in his mind would cost him dearly, but for her, he was willing to do it. He was willing to do anything.

"I can," he went on. "Think of it like a video tape. I can record over the worst parts, so that you only have the important bits. Like your father passing. I doubt you wanna relive that memory, much less make your family do so by having to inform you again. But the parts that haunt you, that make it hard to sleep, I can take care of that."

"But - then what about you? Could I still see you?"

He paled slightly, his mouth dry. "I - honestly don't know. I've never modified a memory that directly influenced the reach of a wanderer. I imagine you wouldn't need to wander anymore though, no. But you wouldn't even remember meeting—"

"No." She was vehemently shaking her head. "No, I made it this far. I'm finally healing. I did all the work, and I won't take a shortcut, especially if it means losing you."

"Who knows? Maybe—"

"No, 'Cheron. I won't risk it. I won't risk you, not ever,

and if this plan does that in any way, I would rather let him be."

"It doesn't, not the rest of it, I promise."

"Okay, then the memories stay. And besides, he's the problem now, not the memories, not anymore."

He didn't argue it any further, but he refused to let his own relief at her decision show on his face in case she changed her mind. Instead, he cradled her in his arms, pressing his lips to the crown of her head and pulling the sheets over them. What an odd thing to stumble upon, this fathomless love for a mortal. And what a dangerous thing to fall into.

"What would I have to do?" she questioned after a long while, her fingers curling against his neck.

He inhaled a deep breath. "Just - invite him to a slumber party."

12

PENELOPE

Penelope's anxiety was like a bad odor, permeating the air with the type of strength that made it difficult to breathe. She paced the living room, smoothing her hands down her blouse at random intervals until she resigned to wringing them nonstop. Every now and again, she whispered Acheron's name, gathering strength from the reminder that everything would be fine, that he would be there to protect her when this plan reached its climax. Then he would let her reach hers, and all of this would feel like one terrible nightmare until it felt like nothing at all. She knew nightmares, had been roommates with them for months. What was one more?

Acheron's offer plagued her too, a swelling hope for what it would be like without the terrible memories of the darkest night of her life. But she had made her decision, and she would stick by it. She had earned her freedom from that fear, and she had clawed her way out of that pit of despair. She wasn't going back. And she wasn't giving up Acheron.

The doorbell rang, and she inhaled a sharp breath before slowly exhaling, focusing on the control of her breathing. Wetting her lips, she forced her hands to her sides and made her way towards the door. She opened it to reveal Shane on the doorstep, a backpack slung over his shoulder and a smaller bag in his hand. He smiled at her, his eyes twinkling, and she returned it to the best of her ability as she stepped aside to allow him access. She followed him into the living room, doing everything in her power to maintain her composure. Yet even the scent of his cologne had her on edge, her desire to see this to completion at war with her fight-or-flight instinct. She wanted to get through this quickly.

"I'm glad you called," he said, dropping his bags on the sofa. "You sure you didn't want me to pick up dinner though? I didn't mind."

"No, no, I had already planned on ordering pizza," she assured him. "Actually, it got here before you did. Let me go..."

She gestured to the kitchen, and he nodded. "For sure. You wanna smoke? I can roll one."

"Yeah, that sounds good."

She was swift in her journey to and from the kitchen, unwilling to leave him alone while he prepared something for both of them to smoke. She still had a lower tolerance than him without a doubt, but she hoped that serving him a couple beers with dinner might help alleviate that gap. The sooner he fell asleep tonight, the better.

Setting the pizza down on the coffee table, she sat beside him with a slice of her own, watching as he broke up the green and brown clump of bud sitting on the tray before him.

"I thought you were gonna stay at your mom's?" he asked almost nonchalantly.

"Uh, yeah, I was, but -" She had prepared for this, and

yet, it was difficult to say the words she had rehearsed. They made her physically ill. She forced herself to continue nonetheless. "Look, Shane, I'm sorry for how I've been acting with you. I wasn't angry or anything, at least not with you. I'm - more angry with myself, and I need to learn how to handle things on my own. I have to reclaim my power."

He looked over at her, his eyes searching hers with the most careful of combs. Everything he did felt different now, more malignant than before, like a test she wouldn't dare fail. Now that she knew what she knew —and she was certain she knew it with or without a proper confrontation — there was no going back to the way it was before. There was no seeing him as anything other than a monster.

She suppressed the urge to whither under his gaze, offering an apologetic smile. At last, he returned it.

"I'm sorry for being so pushy. I just wanted to be there for you."

"And I appreciate that." She tried to make sure her smile reached her eyes. "Thank you."

"Of course."

He went on rolling the joint while she searched for a movie to put on, her eyes flickering towards the clock. She was both anxious for and apprehensive of what would inevitably come next, but she did what she could to remain in the moment. When he passed her the joint, she took several generous pulls, allowing the herb to cleanse her of whatever it could. Soon, a curtain of smoke was draped across the room, the distinct scent of the weed complementing the incense burning on the table.

After awhile, they fell into comfortable conversation during the quieter parts of whatever movie they'd chosen, Shane's friendliness morphing into subtle flirting as time went on. She fell in line, following the flow and playing into his little game. She couldn't think to do otherwise, nor could she allow herself to try and unpack who he was beside who she believed him to be before because it would send her spiraling, and she had to see this through. Otherwise, her family —her father— may never know true justice. Besides, even if she was certain of the truth, she wanted to hear him say it.

As the second joint made its rounds, Eli rested his hand on her leg, and she fought the urge to flinch. Instead, she focused on the high and the way the room shifted and changed around her. The smoke rings he created in the air before them were becoming more mesmerizing by the minute, the colors on the TV growing richer and more vibrant. Every now and again, she reminded herself to look at the clock, to keep to the schedule she'd laid out for herself in order to navigate the night. Unnerving as it was, she soothed herself with the image of Acheron she had committed to memory, heavily detailed and hardly doing him any justice. He would come if he had to. She understood that. He had said it. If he had to tear through realms to get to her in the waking world, if he even thought she was in danger, he would come. That was the other reason the schedule was so important. If she was late, Shane might not even get the chance to profess his innocence, and Acheron would have to step into the one place his enemies could reach him. She refused to risk it.

As time wound down to eleven, she was sitting at the peak of a perfect high, her eyelids heavy and her mind muddy. Shane was slumped over beside her, his shoulder against hers, his head so close that she could hear his every inhale and the click of his teeth when he closed his mouth.

It was time. She knew it was time, but it still took her a moment or two in order to gather her bearings, to prepare herself for the last leg of this endeavor. All she had to do was get through this. Just this, and then it would be over.

Pushing herself to her feet, she locked her knees until she was able to ensure her balance. Then she began tidying up the place, breaking down the pizza boxes and throwing away his beer bottles. He watched her from where he sat, and although he didn't move, she could feel his eyes on her back both unfocused and unwavering. When the cleaning was done, she could put it off no longer. She had to get it over with.

Standing at the arm of the couch opposite him, she crossed her arms over her chest.

"Look, I -" She looked down at her feet. "I'm not ready to - *do* anything, but - I was wondering if you would sleep in my bed? With me? Just for tonight?"

He cocked his head, lifting his chin and narrowing his eyes as if seeing her for the first time. She stared right back, firm in her resolve, refusing to give him any hint of her ulterior motives. Truth be told however, she was all but shaking, her nerves shot and her anxiety at a record high.

"You don't have to," she went on, "but - if you wanted..."

His lips twitched. "Of course, Penny, whatever you need."

"Thank you." She breathed a sigh of relief although for what, she wasn't sure. "Come on."

He didn't need to be told twice. Popping up from the couch, he picked up his bags and followed her up the stairs once she shut off the TV and made sure the security system was armed. The house settled into a cool quiet, the only sound being their footfalls in the second floor hallway. The weed in her system kept her hands firm on the reins of her composure, her heartbeat slowing and her breathing shallow. When they entered the bedroom, she busied herself with gathering her pajamas.

"Left side is mine," she informed him, her tone playful. "I'm gonna change."

He nodded as she hurried into the bathroom, locking the door behind her. She took her time brushing her teeth and combing out her hair, staring into the mirror and silently soothing herself. In the corner of her eye, a shadow lurked, something that once gave her great grief. However, now, it was the only comfort she had. And it was the most effective. All she had to do was lay down beside him. All she had to do was fall asleep.

Acheron said it didn't matter if Shane fell asleep too, but it mattered to her. She did not trust him, not anymore, and the thought of leaving her body alone with him terrified her especially after how lenient she had been all night. But Acheron had sworn no harm would come to her, that Shane wouldn't have the chance, and she believed him. She had to.

He was already laying down in the bed when she exited the bathroom, his bare shoulders peering out from beneath the comforter and a warm smile on his face. She returned it, sitting down on her side and plugging her phone into the charger. She had already set it to record all audio, a failsafe she felt was necessary although she wasn't sure what good it might do if all went awry. It made her feel better though, and at the moment, that was all she could hope for.

Taking up her pen, she took a long drag before offering it to Shane. He took it with a nod of gratitude, and she settled beneath the covers while he was preoccupied with his hit. She had opted for a pair of baggy sweats and a long-sleeve tee, but even so, she curled in on herself to the best of her ability, her back to him. When he leaned over her to return the pen, she fought the urge to recoil. With a shaking hand, she took it from him and placed it back on the bedside table. His return to his side of the bed was slow, slower than it needed to be, and when she turned out the lamp, a chill ran through her. She felt more vulnerable than she ever had. Acheron's first appearance to her, the moment she realized she wasn't alone in her room the night of her father's death, neither of those moments held a candle to this one.

Just go to sleep.

But sleep wouldn't come. She wrestled with it, and she pleaded with it, and she bared her teeth, but it refused to settle. Shane's soft snores after an hour or so were of no comfort either, his weight beside her all but suffocating. She had to go to sleep in order to end this though. If she failed, it would all be for nothing.

Slipping out of bed quietly, she went back into the bathroom, digging out the sleeping pills from the medicine cabinet. Tossing one into her mouth, she washed it down with water from the tap then returned to bed, attempting to focus on what would be rather than what was. Shutting her eyes, she fixated on the sound of Acheron's voice, the cruel cut of his antlers, the hulking vastness of his chiseled form, the glint in his blood red eyes, and the way his hands felt on her skin.

Penelope...

His voice wrapped around her like the warmest blanket, easing away the restlessness in her limbs and coaxing her into some semblance of comfort. She allowed it to, eagerly so, nestling into the memory of him and willing herself closer to his warmth. She didn't know how long it took or when it happened. She just knew that at some point, she blinked, and like so many other nights since meeting her demon, when she opened her eyes again, she was in her room but not in her room.

She had learned how to tell the difference between Acheron's world and the waking world. In his realm, the colors were pale, the shadows were deeper, and she felt weightless amidst it all even when she was pinned down where she lay. However, despite knowing without a shadow of a doubt that she was in his realm, she saw no sign of her demon. The dark patches in the corners of the room did not grow. They did not ebb and flow and shake and evolve. They did not unveil him once her eyes focused. He simply - wasn't there.

She feared calling his name because she wasn't sure if it would summon him or just wake her up. Turning to her side, she found Shane there beside her, fast asleep and as solid as ever, the way Jenna had been the first time Penelope experienced sleep paralysis. She wondered how it worked, how she would be able to reach him here, how Acheron would, but Acheron had assured her it was possible. He reminded her that she was in control, and she was once more forced to wonder if he truly *was* a manifestation of her mind, someone to say all the things she wanted to hear. She sure hoped not. This was not a plan she would have followed through with on her own. More specifically, it was not a plan that she *could* follow through with on her own.

"Shane?" It was little more than a whisper at first. "Shane."

He didn't stir. There was nothing to convince her that he could hear her at all. Yet, when she reached out and took hold of his shoulder, pleading in her mind for this to work, he abruptly sat upright with eyes wide open and his jaw slack, a gasp escaping him. Several blinks, and he looked over at her, confusion and question in his stare.

"Penny? What's wrong?"

She expected her fear to overwhelm her, to take her by the tongue and submerge her into silence until her lungs gave out. Instead, the anger and disgust that had been sitting stagnant in her belly began to simmer there. Then boil. And something told her it wasn't just her anger she was feeling.

She got out of bed, standing at its side to face him with hands crossed over her chest. He gave her a bewildered look, which only strengthened her resolve, not that it had withered much in the moments they had spent together. But in this light, in this dark and dim and unflattering light, she could see him for exactly what he was. His features were distorted, his skin a sheet of milky white, his edges blurred...

A night terror.

"Did - did I do something?" he asked.

Then she felt it. *Him*, stretching out on all sides of her like an oil spill, Shane's mere presence a match tossed into it to set the room alight.

Confront him.

She straightened, rolling her shoulders.

"You tell me, Shane."

Her voice carried like hooves beating against the ground, the warning evident in the words.

Shane gawked at her. "I - I don't know. I—"

"You were there that night, weren't you? In my house? In my room?"

HIs eyes widened further, mouth opening and closing,

his face sheet white. His features grew more grotesque by the moment.

"Wh - what? Penny—"

"That's how they knew where everything was, how they knew about the money, how you knew about my watch. You knew. You knew everything, and you told them."

"Penny, that's not - no. No, I didn't— I—"

His eyes threatened to bulge out of his head now, and she need not look over her shoulder to know what it was that had him spooked. She could feel the growing presence there at her back, fueled with wrath and horrendous intentions. She fed off of it, letting it carry her forward.

"Just tell me why, Shane." Her voice remained soft, almost sympathetic. "Tell me why you did it."

"Penny..." He shook his head, looking down at his hands before quickly trying to jump out of the bed. Before he could put a foot on the ground, he was slammed back down onto the mattress by an invisible force, pinning him to it the way she had been pinned to it so many times.

"What the fuck?" he yelped, looking down at his useless body. "Penny! What the fuck is this! What—"

She moved around the bed slowly, and Acheron moved with her, not yet fully formed but certainly fully present. She had never felt stronger.

"You are not leaving here until you tell me the truth, Shane."

"Penny, please." Acheron's shadow fell over him. "Please! What the fuck!"

"What did you do!" she demanded, her demon's wrath magnifying her own. "Tell me what you did, and tell me why you did it!"

The shadow reached his face, darkening around his throat, and it was almost as though he was compelled to speak. “I was drowning! I - I needed the money! Just to get a place and - and get this certificate! I was gonna pay you back—”

“You broke into my house! You took everything from me! And you killed my father!”

“I didn’t do that! I didn’t kill him! Look, I - I went into your room to make sure they didn’t do anything to you! I - I didn’t know your dad would be there!”

“You took my sense of safety! You have watched me struggle to sleep for months!”

Shane screamed. He screamed at the top of his lungs, and she basked in the sound. Her vision was tinted red and blurred by unbridled fury, but as she looked down on him, she could clearly see the thick gashes now appearing across his bare torso. It did not shake her. It had no effect on her at all.

No, that was a lie. She liked the sight of it. *Enjoyed* it.

“I’m sorry!” Shane wailed. “I’m so sorry! I never meant for that to happen. I - my dad cut me off. I needed the money to survive. I—”

“And you didn’t think to ask for help! To come to me first before you decided to bring my life crashing down!”

“I - I would’ve. I wanted to, but - I - I was drunk, and I let it slip about the money to Dwayne, and - and after that, he wouldn’t get off of it! He would’ve done it with or without me! I went to protect you!”

Dwayne. Dwayne Lockner. She knew the name from the reports, from the paper, from one of the very few calls she got from the cops. Officer Doren called him the trigger man. Penelope called him a dead man.

“He died because of you,” she said, her voice low and acidic. She stepped closer to him, the shadow cast across his immobile body growing ever darker. "You killed him. You did this."

"Penny, please, I—"

"And then you tried to move in on me. You kept coming around. Even when I asked for space, even when I made excuse after excuse, you wouldn't listen!"

Another gash opened up along the middle of his chest. Everything was red. And blurry. Very blurry.

"I am sorry! I am sorry, Penny, please!"

"You killed him! You fucking killed him! You took him from me!"

It all caught up with her then. Her knees buckled, and she collapsed to the floor, her chest threatening to crack open just like his. Then there was a warmth at her back, and Shane was shrieking like a banshee. Acheron's hand fell against her spine, his lips brushing over the shell of her ear. She wanted to scramble into his arms, to cling to him like a scared child and never let go. Before she could though, he was standing up.

Let me finish this first, Princess, he hissed into her head, causing her sobs to stagger.

She lifted her gaze, watching him stalk forward to the amplified panic of his knowing victim. Acheron's antlers seemed larger than ever, his tail flicking behind him and his black skin looking like solid metal. He took a deep breath, almost as though he were smelling the air...

Oh. He was *feeding*. He was feeding off of Shane's fear.

Shane screamed himself hoarse and worked himself ragged against his bindings, but it was all futile to his cause. Acheron held a hand over his bleeding chest, not quite touching, but the effect was evident regardless. Shane was shrinking right before her eyes, the minimal color he had left in his face draining fast and the blood streaming down his sides growing thick and dark. Then, when he was clinging to life, Acheron seemed to stop what he was doing, kneeling down beside the bed and taking hold of Shane's chin. He guided the man's gaze to his own, his lips curling.

"Where you're going, you will never have to worry about money again." Shane whimpered, but Acheron held firm to his jaw.

"I'm - sorry. Penny..."

"You will be."

It was sudden. A beat of silence, Then the deafening sound of flesh tearing and bones shattering, shortly accompanied by Shane's gurgling. She couldn't look away. She couldn't justify stopping it. Watching Shane, her friend, be torn apart didn't phase her in any way. All she could do was hope that his pain was greater than hers, than her father's, and that it would last long after he was cleansed from her sheets.

"It will," Acheron answered her. "You have my word."

He whipped his hand down on Shane, but Penelope didn't see it make contact. In the blink of her eyes, Shane — and all traces of him— were gone. The blood, the sweat, the smell of piss; it was all gone. Acheron turned back to her, and the moment he was in reach, she launched herself into his arms. He caught her and held her tight to him, running his hand through her hair.

"It's alright now, Princess, don't worry."

He moved towards the opposite side of the bed, ascending into the air long enough to position himself in a sitting position against the headboard.

"Where is he?" she croaked.

"Enduring every kind of pain imaginable. You will never have to see him again."

She shook her head. "I - did I do that? The cuts on his

chest?"

He immediately shook his own although when she looked up in his eyes, he wouldn't meet hers. "No, I did that."

"But I gave you permission, didn't I? To touch him? That's how it worked. I invited him into my dream, and I gave you permission to touch him." *To hurt him.*

"I did it."

"You told me that I have all the control here, that all I need to do is say the word."

"And that's true, but I am not yet bound to you. I have my free will just as you have yours."

She opened her mouth to retaliate once more, but she wasn't sure what else to say. He frowned.

"Penelope, this wasn't your fault, and you aren't the villain here. If you would've handled it the mortal way, he would have never seen justice. It would have been your word against his, and from what I know of your world, men that look like him get away with a whole lot worse. What I did, I did for your safety. For your peace, and I would do it again. If you asked me to, I would find a way to gut the other three too."

She quickly rejected the idea —or rather, stowed it away for another time— but she knew he was right. Shane would have never seen a courtroom. Cut off or not, he came from an affluent White family with a bright future and old enough money. And she was a woman of color who suffered from night terrors after just losing her father. They had already concluded she'd made up the fourth participant. Her paranoia would have been weaponized, his kindness a shield against her claims. Who would have believed her? Who would have cared? No one. No one except Acheron.

"Thank you," she breathed.

He tightened his hold on her. "You never have to thank me. I will burn this entire world and the next to the ground before I let anyone hurt you again."

And regardless of their probability, she meant her next words just the same. "As I would do for you."

He smiled, pressing his lips to her forehead. "Let us hope it never comes to that."

13

ACHERON

Acheron's blood was finally beginning to cool, indignation seeping from his skin at a gradual pace. He enclosed himself and Penelope in the wrap of his wings, shielding her from the room she had just watched a man die in. In the waking world at least. Shane would live forever in The Fires' deepest pits, jumping from horror to horror like a new brand of circuit training. The bastard was lucky Acheron hadn't had more time, or more patience. Despite this eternal imprisonment, his death had been quicker than he deserved for what he had done, and Acheron refused to apologize. There was nothing wrong with being monstrous when it was in defense of those you love.

A reality he would not be unpacking any time soon, by the way.

His tail snaked up between them, finding her pressure points and using them to calm her spirit. He froze when he felt her hand wrap around it, offering a gentle squeeze before she glanced up at him.

"What does it feel like? When I touch your tail?"

He smirked. "Like you're stroking my cock."

"Really?" A look of pure curiosity graced her face, her hand sliding slowly along his tail. His eye twitched. "Exactly like I'm stroking it or just kinda?"

"Depends how thorough you— fuck."

She gave it a firm tug, squeezing and stroking in a rhythmic fashion as she turned to face him more fully. He immediately took hold of her hips, lifting her up and guiding her down to straddle his lap so that his tail was between her legs. With a wave of his hand, he relieved her of the pajamas she had no doubt chosen specifically for her unwanted slumber party. He reached for one of her nipples, tweaking it idly between his fingers and earning himself a hiss and another sharp pull on his tail. Of course, that stimulated her just as well, the smooth skin rubbing along her pussy lips and making her wind down onto him further.

"Mm, already you want me to take you apart again?" he teased, palming her ass and sinking his claws into it until she squealed. "Always so needy. We can't even play your favorite game anymore, can we? You can't even pretend you don't want me to fuck your pretty little brains out."

She wanted to try though. He could see it in her eyes, read it in her head, but then he dipped a finger down lower and hooked it into the edge of her entrance, and she withered in his arms. The tip of his tail dusted the side of her face, her jaw, the edge of her lips. His wings caressed her back, every inch of him both stimulated and eager to stimulate. He groaned as his cock rose beneath her, both of his hands moving lower so that his fingers could spread her lips and open her up.

"Cheron."

Her eyes fluttered shut as his tail probed her mouth, and when she clamped down on it, he bucked his hips upward.

He watched her suck him harder, deeper, her free hand reaching between them to play with her clit. A hiss escaped him, his desire to continue watching her at war with his desire to flip her over and fuck her until the bedframe cracked beneath the force of it. He opted for a compromise, lifting her up once more so that he could impale her upon his shaft, the high-pitched howl she released shooting straight through to his balls.

"Fuck!"

"Did that fill you up?" he challenged. "Or do you still need more?"

"More." It was instantaneous. "More, please!"

"Tell me. Tell me you want me to fuck you."

"I want you to fuck me."

"Again."

"I want you to fuck me!"

He threaded his fingers in her hair, gripping hard as he brought her face close to his. "Tell me you want me to fuck you like the filthy little slut you are."

"I do. I do."

"*Say* it."

She was panting already, and when she tried to move her hips, his other hand pinned her in place.

"Say it, or I will leave you right here, whining and begging for this cock."

A whimper. "I - I want you to fuck me like - like the filthy little *slut* I am."

He made quick work of her first orgasm, bouncing her up and down on his cock with unbridled ease once he got his hands back under her ass. And she was more eager than ever to take every inch he was willing to afford her. All the while, she continued stroking him, earning hiss after grunt after groan that only served to fuel his pace beneath her.

Soon, his tail was snaking around her throat, tightening just enough to make her eyes roll back and her breathing stall. The denial of air mixed with the shattering thrust into her cunt was the perfect recipe for a delicious disaster, and within minutes, she was coming apart, her body seizing so hard that he had to hold her upright and in place. Even so, once he relinquished his hold on her throat, she slumped backwards with a panting moan.

"Aw, too much for you, Princess? All worn out already? Tsk, tsk, I thought we were building your tolerance, not destroying it."

"Please..."

"Please what? Go easy on you? Give you a break? I'm not done with this pretty little cunt yet. I'm still hard, and I'm going to cum. If I have to hold you down and use you like a fucking toy, I will."

She seemed to garner the initiation of the game rather quickly, her body gathering the dregs of her energy to try and escape him. She squirmed, twisting herself around onto her stomach and trying to scramble down the bed. He chuckled, lunging forward onto her back and pinning her down with a hand between her shoulders.

"No," she whimpered, gripping the footboard.

"It's of no use, Penny. You know that."

"Let me go!"

"You know what you have to do, what you have to say."

"No!"

"Mhmm."

Unfurling his tongue, he let it dip into the seam of her ass, slowly descending towards her hole. She shuddered under his touch, a string of useless pleas spilling out onto the sheets her face was now pressed into. He whipped his hand hard across her ass, devouring the cry it earned him, before he began to rim her entrance.

I don't think we've played with this hole enough, Princess.

Spoken directly into her mind, the tone of his voice dropped several octaves, weighed down by his growing arousal.

"No," she moaned. "You can't. You won't."

"I can, and I will. There will be no inch of you that has not known every inch of me, Penny. There will be no place in your being that I will not mark as my own. That, I can assure you."

He slid his tongue into her, probing and stretching and preparing her for what he planned to do next. She continued to writhe and fight, to try and pull herself free with the help of the footboard gripped so hard in her hands that the wood creaked. She clenched around him, and he rewarded her performance with the tuck of his tail between the sheets and her clit. A surprised gasp left her.

She looked divine beneath him, her body drawn taut as a bowstring with every muscle flexing and rolling beneath her chestnut skin. He retracted his tongue, leaning forward over her and allowing the swollen head of his shaft to drag heavily between her cheeks. Grinding down into the seam, his breathing grew heavy, anticipation roiling in his gut.

"Oh, the things I'm going to do to you, Princess."

All she could do in return was yelp.

He moved his hand up to the back of her neck, pinning her in place while he sunk into her inch by expanding inch. Her feet and upper body came clear off of the bed while her torso arched into it. He spread her open with his other hand, his eyes fixed on the way her muscles contracted the deeper he entered her.

He himself trembled with the sensation, his cock already claimed in a vice grip. Once he was down to the hilt, he gave her a few precious seconds to adjust, to assimilate, before thrusting his tail into her pussy. In the moments of shock that she confronted this feeling with, he drew up his hips and slammed them right back down, the shrill scream that ricocheted around the room imprinting on his skin with a coveted heat.

"That's a good girl, hm?"

"No - no no no, stop!"

"Make me stop, Penelope. I dare you." She whimpered. "You won't, will you? My eager little slut. You can't. You need this. You need me to fuck you."

"No—"

"You need me to cum inside you, to make you scream."

"No!"

"And you need me to take you by force so you don't have to admit how badly you want my cock inside you."

She pulled harder on the footboard, the wood bowing towards her. It was an effort made in vain, and they both knew it. And neither of them cared. She kept trying.

"You - monster!"

He rammed his cock into her again.

"*Your* monster."

The faster he fucked her, the harder she cried, but he could feel the real resistance strong in her mind. She wouldn't say his name. She wouldn't ask for mercy. She refused. It only made him want to test her further.

Taking hold of both of her arms at the elbow, he yanked her up and onto her knees, his tail and his dick alternating their thrusts. She was tied up in one long scream, at his mercy and drunk with need. Her second orgasm took them both by surprise, her spine locking up and her legs shaking. He didn't stop, maintaining his hold on her as well as his pace. The mere scent of her pleasure tightened the coil in his belly however, its inebriating effect spurring him on further. He was so deeply submerged in his own euphoria that he was losing control of himself, his wings stretched from wall to wall and his antlers sharp as needles. It had been evident from the beginning. Whatever he took from her, he was twice as willing to give back tenfold, and he had. Again and again, he had offered the softest parts of himself to her albeit in the most aggressive ways, and he regretted nothing. Being inside her was worth far more than he had paid up to now.

Her third orgasm left her limp in his arms, her sharp cries sanded down to hoarse yelps and withering groans. She still refused to demand mercy, but he knew her limitations by now as well as his own, and with all of her ecstasy in the air around him, he was struggling to hold on as well. He pumped into her with thrusts that struck like lightning, each more devastating than the last, his hands gripping her by the shoulders and shoving her down into the mattress.

"Cheron..." It was little more than a faint mutter.

"Just a little more... That's a good girl."

"No..."

"But you take it so well."

She reached out for the footboard once more. He gritted his teeth and hammered away at her ass until the pressure became too much. There was no warning, no real awareness of its arrival. His orgasm merely swept him up like a tidal wave, her muscles squeezing him hard and milking him dry. His thrusts grew shorter, quicker, more wild, desperation in every one.

"Fuck!"

His hands fell upon hers, both of them clinging to the board as he bottomed out thrice in quick succession, his cum filling her before it spattered across her cheeks and his stomach. She was humming too, squirting like a faucet, her body no longer her own, contorting beneath him as though she were possessed. Maybe, in a way, she was.

He collapsed atop her, kissing her neck with a bruising insistence. She reached back with a weak hand, gripping one of his antlers with a weary moan.

What a good girl.

Another moan, her hips winding against his even as her eyes fell shut and her breathing slowed. As much as he wanted her again, he doubted she would last through it, and the last thing he wanted was for her to disappear halfway through another climax. He wrapped her in his arms, lifting them both up into the air so as to place them back at the head of the bed. He lay on his side, holding her in his arms, and she turned to burrow her face in his chest.

"Will it always be like this?" she mumbled.

"The sex? I sure hope so."

A soft fist hit his collarbone. "No, not the sex."

He snickered before sifting through her thoughts. "Ah, you mean the seeing each other here. Well, it doesn't—"

It was subtle. The shift in the air, the dim of the room, the pressure at the back of his neck. Such an unusual feeling, such an uncommon sensation, he almost didn't recognize it until it was too late. But he did, he did, and the dread that filled him was enough to propel him from the bed.

When he turned back to her, Penelope was sitting upright, staring at him with confusion in her eyes.

"What is it?"

"Say my name," he said.

"What?"

"Say my name." His voice grew more urgent.

"Why? We—"

"Say it!"

"Cheron, we—"

"Penelope." He darted forward, gripping her shoulders. "I need you to wake up right now. Right this instant. I do not have time to explain, and I need you to trust me."

He gave her a firm kiss on the mouth before stepping back again, and although the consternation remained, she nodded slowly. And said his name.

Instantly, the room blurred and lurched like an accelerating train until he was back in his own chambers. Rushing towards the door, he jumped right back when he found a figure standing directly on the other side of it, cloaked like a wraith in dark robes, his antlers so wide that they extended past the frame of the archway. He lifted his head, blood red eyes mirroring Acheron's.

"Good, you made it," Belphegor stated in a deep, reverberating voice. "We have to talk, Acheron."

Acheron exhaled. "You're right. We do."

14

PENELOPE

Three days. It had been three days since she'd seen Acheron, since she'd even been able to sleep much less dream. Something always seemed to catch her just before she sunk deep enough to reach him, and calling his name into the void proved futile each and every time. Dread ran through her and nothing much else, a constant anxiety wreaking havoc on her functioning. Getting out of bed was nearly impossible despite the lack of rest, and the world seemed more dim than ever. Where had he gone? What had happened to make him so panicked in their last moments together?

On top of missing him, Penelope was also grappling with the fact that Shane was gone. Like really gone. There was no trace of him in the house, his car no longer in the driveway and even the scent of his cologne wiped from her sheets. The place beside her had been undisturbed when she'd awoken after, and everything from the beer bottles he'd indulged in to the joint roaches he'd left in the makeshift ashtray downstairs were gone. It was like he'd never been there at all. No one ever came looking. No one asked any questions, not even when news of his disappearance aired on TV and appeared in the paper, publicity her father never got. Any other time, she might feel something more akin to guilt, but at the moment, the only thing she knew was grief. The only loss she knew was Acheron.

She sat at the edge of her bed, chewing her thumbnail and staring at the bottle of sleeping pills on her nightstand. She hadn't tried taking them, hadn't wanted to resort to that after doing so the night of Shane's confession. Her phone was ringing beside her, Jenna's face smiling up at her, but she opted not to answer. They had spoken that morning, and Penelope had forced herself to inform Jenna of Shane's disappearance so that she wouldn't be caught off guard when she returned home. And right now, Penelope couldn't focus on some mundane conversation about how she was doing or what she was feeling regarding the situation. She was too busy weighing the pros and cons of her addiction to a demon.

Picking up the bottle, she let the sound of the tablets rattling within soothe her. Tossing her phone to the other side of the bed, she laid down on her back, staring at the label. She had to see him. She had to know what had happened. The look in his eyes right before she left him last, the sheer terror that resided there. It terrified her too. Anything that could make a demon look that way definitely should.

And why had she not been able to sleep since? No matter how high she got or how much wine she had at dinner, something kept pulling her back. She had to break through that barrier, whatever it was. She had to get back to him. It wasn't about the pills. It wasn't about sleep. It was about him.

Opening the lid, she slipped her index and middle finger

inside, scooping out two tablets. Trading the pill bottle for her water bottle, she took both of them and laid back down, trying to clear her mind of any and all distractions. That was easy enough. The only thing she had the capacity to think about anyway was Acheron, and she fought off the worry that came with wondering what it was she would be sinking into if this worked. Shutting her eyes, she uttered his name into the dark repeatedly until her lips refused to move and her body sunk into the mattress. And then deeper.

She felt it somewhere in the darkness, the tug from within her ribcage. It was as though something had hooked into her, trying to drag her back to the surface. She fought it to the best of her ability, sinking further into the black abyss below until at last, the tie broke free. Her eyes shut again, and when they opened this time, she was in her room but not in her room. She was here. She was in his realm.

Before she had the chance to wonder where he was, he appeared beside her on the bed, sitting at its edge with a relieved smile on his face.

"You know you can't spend your whole life in bed, right, Princess?"

She scrunched her nose at the new nickname, but that was all she could afford as she launched herself straight into his arms. He caught her with ease, his arms wrapping tight around her until it was all that was holding her together. She didn't know she was crying until his tail came up to wipe the moisture from her eyes, his lips pressing into the crown of her head.

"What happened?" she croaked, nuzzling into his neck.

He sighed heavily but didn't answer, burrowing his face into her hair. She didn't mind the extra few minutes to bask in his presence. The weight of missing him was more evident than ever now, rivaled only by the elation she felt being in his arms again. She loved him. She knew that to be true, logic be damned. Losing him was not an option she would dare to entertain, not now and not ever.

Pulling back, she looked up at him, her gaze expectant. He gave her one of sincere apology before settling her down on his lap.

"The Dominion," he began, wetting his lips. "They must have sensed something after - Shane, and they were... They got too close for comfort, and I knew if they found us, if they breached the veil, they wouldn't care for excuses. They wouldn't condone what I did."

"So you're in trouble? Because of what I made you do?"

"Penelope, I already told you. You didn't make me do anything. They would have detected something eventually. The way we see each other, there's a breach in the veil. *Their* veil. It was only a matter of time."

"But the blood on your hands would be their excuse."

"They would've found another. I told you. Things are different now. Their rules are different."

"So - what does that mean? Are they why I couldn't get to you these past few nights?"

He shook his head. "My - overseer, my creator, he thought it best I wait a few days. Things are -" He rubbed at his eyes, and to her, he had never looked more human. "They're going to get worse, Penny. The Dominion aren't fucking around anymore. Something's wrong up there, and we don't know what it is. We just know they're gunning for us in any way they can, and that can only lead to one thing."

"... And - us? The - mortals?"

He swallowed.

"Acheron, I can't - I cannot lose you."

"And you cannot waste your life here, in this realm. He's gone now, and I know that doesn't bring your father back, but the world is a little bit safer for you at least, and you should enjoy it."

"I don't want to enjoy it without you! Don't you get that!"

"Penelope..."

"You asked me if I wanted to erase the memory, and what did I say? I am in control. You told me that over and over again, so how is that suddenly not the case anymore?"

He brushed hair from her face as she pouted like a petulant child, eyebrows cast downward. She smacked his hand away.

"Don't treat me like some foolish little girl," she snapped despite her own behavior. "I said it, and I meant it. I do not want to be without you."

"There will be other men, human men, who can—"

"No, there won't, and you know it. And don't sit here and pretend that you can just let me go when the whole reason you showed yourself to me in the first place was because you felt something. So if you don't anymore, you own up to it, but don't—"

"Hey." He gripped her chin, yanking it towards his own. "I feel everything for you, all the things I was never meant to feel. And that is exactly why I cannot sit here and let you waste away in this bed."

"Then come with me."

"I can't do that, Penelope, you know—"

"You said in the beginning that because I knew your name, I could summon you or send you away. I haven't been able to summon you, so there is something you are not telling me."

"Penny, that's—"

"*And* the other night, you said you weren't *yet* bound to me. You made it sound like that was an option. What did it mean?"

She had been analyzing every word he had ever said to her over the past three days, and she knew there had to be a way. She refused to believe otherwise. She stared at him, almost accusatory, and waited. He expelled another heavy sigh.

"To bind a mortal soul to a demon is - it's archaic and it costs each of us at least some of our control. And we don't—"

"Will I be able to see you when I'm awake, yes or no?"

"Yes, but Penelope—"

"And will they - the Dominion - be able to tear us apart? Will they be able to do anything about it?"

"No, but—"

"Then I want to do it."

"You have your whole life ahead of you. What happens when you don't need me anymore? When the trauma is healed and the nightmares are gone?"

"Acheron, I love you. I—"

They both froze, eyes widening as they stared at one another. But neither disappeared. Nothing changed. She was still as solid as she always was, and so was he. She reached up to make sure anyway, cupping his face in her hands. He simply nodded, a look of impressed disbelief etched in his features.

"How did - what's happening?" she whispered.

"You're serious, aren't you?"

She paused a moment. "About keeping you with me? I've never been more serious in my entire life... But - what does that have to do with... am I trapped?"

He shook his head with a wry smile. "No, no. It's - it's about intent. You can say my name without leaving because you don't want to leave, but before, you couldn't control it.

You didn't know how, and I had no clue how to teach you because I've never had to."

"You didn't tell me that."

"I didn't tell you a lot of things, Penelope, because I realized that coming to you in the first place was selfish. My feelings for you never should have influenced my judgment, but - I've never had any before so I didn't know what to do with them."

"I'm glad you didn't then because I don't regret any of it, and I will do whatever it takes to stay with you. So tell me what to do."

It was his turn to stare at her, searching her mind, body, **AND** soul for any signs of doubt, of uncertainty, of any reason not to oblige her. But she knew her heart, and she knew her soul as well. She could feel every single one of his emotions, sense every single intention he had, read every word he left unsaid right off of his face. Or in his touch. They were already bound in every way but one, and judging by the way his expression softened, he knew it too.

"You're sure?" he questioned. It was half hearted at best.

"I'm sure." It was unwavering from start to finish.

He nodded. "Then I guess we'll need a Reaper."

IN ALL OF their nights together in her spirit room, she had never once thought to ask if she was able to leave it. She also had never noticed just how translucent her skin was here. However, as they walked down the road at the center of Acheron's city, it was evident that she was hardly solid at all despite the lack of a proper sun. The sky was the deepest crimson, the moon that adorned it gleaming like an onyx stone amidst heather grey clouds. Acheron held her hand in his own, leading her along while she surveyed her surroundings in boundless awe. Apart from the natural lighting, this looked every bit like a city that could very well exist in her realm. There were demons —some that looked similar to Acheron and others with horns like rams and antelopes and bulls. Then there were mortals. Or she supposed mortal souls, just like her, and despite the opacity of their skin being roughly 60% or so, they looked no different from people in the waking world.

"You'll be able to come here as you wish once we are bound," he explained.

"So - like a visa? Like when people from different countries get married?"

He took a moment before nodding. "Something like that. We'll both have dual citizenship then, and you can move more freely through worlds. You'll still have to do so in your sleep, but you'll be far more lucid and far harder to wake up, so we'll be mindful of that."

"If - if either of us is harmed in the waking world, what happens?"

"It depends on the wound, but - if you mean by The Dominion, they won't hurt mortals. And I can come home and hopefully be healed. My friend I told you about, Xaphan, that's who we're going to see. He's still in the infirmary, but he's recovering."

"So he fought them off? The ones who attacked them."

Acheron's features darkened. "I'm sure if they meant to kill him, they would have, so I have to be very careful when I am in the waking world, even if it's just in your bedroom."

"You - do you—"

She waited for him to read the question from her mind, and once he did, he smiled and nodded. "I do have a human form, but I will need to go to Belphegor to have it - tailored."

She raised a brow. "Like a suit?"

"Exactly like a suit." He grinned wider. "See, the human form I have currently is - it's fragile and temporary. It's only meant for swift concealment, and much of my power is suppressed when I use it. Of course, I've never had to use it because I don't go into the waking world, but if ever I had to for any reason-"

"Like war?"

He nodded. "Like war, I have it on hand. However, seeing as my trips might become more extensive, he'll need to ensure it's strong enough to encapsulate my true form."

She leaned into him. "You'll only need it if we have to see other people. I don't want you to change."

He smirked over at her. "So you like fucking the monster then, do you?"

"Very much so. In fact, I imagine it's the only reason I like fucking you at all."

He scoffed, and she giggled into his arm, feeling like a smitten teenager. It was half true though. She loved him, and that was for all that he was, but she also knew that the sex was as good as it was because of all the things he could do with all of his perfect appendages. She didn't want a human. She wanted her demon and her demon alone.

"And what if you find me handsome in my human form?" he urged.

"I probably will because it's still you, and I'll take you to dinner or to meet my mother, but I will not go to bed with a mask, Acheron, not ever. You are my monster, remember?"

His smile was genuine now. "That I am, Princess."

They arrived at an oddly shaped building shortly thereafter. To her, it looked sort of like the pictures of DNA in her biology textbooks although it was solid black, the windows tinted to midnight and indiscernible from the rest of the walls. It crawled up into the air like the neck of a great dragon, disappearing far beyond the red dome around them.

"This is - your hospital?"

"Of sorts, yeah," he replied.

"Do you have, like, healer demons?"

"Uh, witches actually."

She whipped her head around to look at him so hard that her neck popped. "Witches?"

His lips quirked. "Your world is much bigger than you could even imagine, Penny. They are one of very few creatures who have an open passport between realms. Except Heaven of course. Most of us steer clear of those gates."

"How many realms are there?"

"There are the major three, but in those three are many others. Heaven, Earth, and Hell are more like subdivisions of each of them."

"What else is - in the same realm as Earth?"

"Apart from the many planets and solar systems and universes? Plenty that exist in that grey area between one realm and the next. That's where things like your ghosts come from. I'll give you a full lesson soon enough. For now, come on. You'll be waking up soon enough, so we have to hurry."

They ventured inside, boarding an elevator that took them up several floors. Nervous energy roiled in her stomach, but it was tangled with excitement. She was not afraid. She was not having second thoughts. This was what she wanted. It had not been long, not at all, but she had been absolutely honest when she'd said she had never been more sure of anything. What had been missing with Shane — before she knew what he was— and every other mortal she had dated wasn't missing with Acheron. He completed her, and she knew it to be true because the nightmares had stopped weeks ago. She had been able to sleep without substances on multiple occasions, but she only felt whole when she was with him. And she had never felt whole before in her lifetime, certainly not after her father passed, but she did now. That was all she needed to know.

When they walked off of the elevator, they entered a hall that looked much like the sky outside, crimson walls with darkened doors lining them. There were twists and turns everywhere throughout rather than just a straight pathway, but Acheron seemed to know his way around. However, halfway down the current hall, they were abruptly intercepted by a large figure that seemed to fill the space from wall to wall, his antlers much the same and mirroring Acheron's. He said demons like him sported those types of horns, but this demon was slightly different from hers. His skin wasn't a bottomless obsidian. It more closely resembled burning coals, hints of dusted grey and warm red undertones. Acheron immediately bowed his head, and on instinct, Penelope did the same. She could feel it. This was Belphegor.

"Acheron," Belphegor said in a deep, rumbling voice. "You've come to see Xaphan."

Acheron nodded. "Yes."

"I'm afraid he's resting. We had a bit of a scare this morning."

"What?" Acheron tensed. "What happened?"

Belphegor beckoned them closer, and Acheron moved so fast that she vaguely wondered if Belphegor had done more than just gesture at them. He led them through one of the many doors lining the left wall and into a room that was much larger than Penelope had expected. There were no light fixtures, but it was bright and fully visible nonetheless. There were a few beds towards the back, a couch and two tables closer to the door, and some chairs along the wall. Though something about them seemed off, like they didn't actually belong here in this room. Belphegor shut the door behind them with a wave of his hand.

"A piece of one of the Dominion's blades was still buried in his thigh. We missed it. We think it was purposely done so that he would die after giving us the message."

"What message?" she questioned before she realized she was speaking.

Belphegor smiled at her. His facial features were also much like Acheron's, thick lips, deep set eyes, sharp teeth that glinted when he opened his mouth, and a sharp, angular face. Still, she could see and feel his power, which seemed to fill the entire room.

"This is her, your wanderer?"

"Yes," Acheron answered.

Belphegor held out his hand, and Penelope took it. Instantly, a cool calm fell over her followed by the sudden ignition of a flame in her belly. She felt - powerful, like she could do anything, like she could do *everything*. It was an odd feeling but not at all unkind.

"It's a pleasure to meet you, Penelope," Belphegor said softly before releasing her hand. "I've heard a lot about you. I wish we could have met during happier times, but unfortunately, the Dominion did not leave Xaphan alive out of the kindness of their hearts. They wanted us to know we were no longer a protected population in your realm. On Earth."

"Were you before? We've always been taught that - demons were, you know..."

"Oh, we know, but before, Earth was a neutral place. As long as the free will of man was honored by both sides, it was always a fair fight for their souls. Sure, we had run-ins every now and again when Heaven fell back from mankind, our kind moved in, but they've never been so aggressive in their endeavors. Now, it would seem that the Dominion would rather pursue war."

"But why? Aren't they supposed to be good? They're like - angels, right?"

Acheron growled "They never cared about being good. They only care about being superior."

"And those are two very different things as you probably know," Belphegor went on. "But for now, we are stable. Xaphan is stable, and we will be prepared for what chaos and madness they induce next."

"But what about mortals?" she pushed. "Do you - will you-"

She wasn't sure what question to ask, but Belphegor seemed to understand. "We have never been interested in claiming a mortal before their time. Death is merely a natural progression, and we never lack souls. Most of our power comes from the living in fact, the things the Dominion and their kind cannot eat. We learned to survive on the scraps. I won't say we're the good guys. We simply know our limitations, and honestly, as you probably can see now, we get along quite well with your people. So when the time comes, we will do what we can to protect man as they are and not as the Dominion would force them to be."

"Even those that think you're evil? That - that think other people are evil or expendable?"

Acheron chuckled now, and Belphegor did as well.

"We're demons, Princess, not superheroes," Acheron returned. "We protect your right to choose, to exist, to be. But we're not going out of our way for every person on Earth. Some of you mortals could do with a bit of hellfire truly. As we know."

She laughed at that despite Shane's face flashing through her mind. "I would agree, and that seems fair."

"As fair as fair gets. That's our motto. Unofficially of course."

She wrapped her arms around his waist without a thought, and he draped his arms over her shoulders, kissing the top of her head. The move was really growing on her.

"So what brings you here then today, Penelope?" Belphegor went on. "Being introduced to the best friend already?"

"Actually." She straightened again, looking between Acheron and Belphegor, the former nodding his head in support. "I want to bind my soul to Acheron's. He doesn't want me to waste away in dreams, but I don't want to live a life without him, so..."

"Ah, so you needed Xaphan. Well, unfortunately, he won't be doing any work of the sort for awhile, but luckily, I can help."

Again, Penelope looked between the two. Acheron squeezed her hand.

"He's the master key," Acheron informed her proudly.

"So...we don't need a reaper?"

"Not for this."

"Come then," Belphegor directed, taking hold of each of their shoulders and turning them to face each other. "The pain will be as minimal as the cut of a blade and the burn of a brand, but you have to commit to it because to undo something like this would be beyond painful for both parties. Do you understand that, Penelope?"

She looked him straight in the eyes. "I do."

"And I have to ask. Were you at all scared or coerced into this binding?"

"No, not at all."

"And you are sure this is what you want?"

She nodded. "I'm sure."

He observed her for what felt like ages, his eyes seemingly looking right through her to somewhere deeper. Once he was satisfied, he nodded again.

"Acheron, your mark."

Acheron moved closer to her, extending the claw on his index finger. It was sharp as a scalpel, and he held it like one, his thumb pressed against the side. He lifted the other hand, gesturing for her to turn around. She did so, refusing to hesitate, to give him any reason to believe she wasn't sure despite him knowing every inch of her mind.

"Are you ready?" His mouth hovered beside her ear.

"Yes," she breathed.

Then he was writing or drawing on her skin, first a circle then a series of smaller shapes she couldn't quite make out. She winced but made no sound, standing patiently as he marked her. It was over in under a minute, but the pressure of his claw was then replaced with the pressure of a finger. It wasn't Acheron's. She knew his touch intricately. And intimately. No, Belphegor seemed to be wiping blood from the wound.

"You can turn around now, Penelope," the elder demon said.

She did so. Acheron was now standing up straight, his chin raised, and Belphegor was drawing a symbol over his chest. In her blood. It began to glow a bright, ruby red, and when it was done, he stepped away. It looked like one of those magic runes she'd seen in books and on the video games she used to play before The Incident. Vaguely, she could make out her first initial. Or at least she thought she could, but she wasn't sure as it looked so foreign. Belphegor took her hand, pressing it against the mark on Belphegor's chest. She felt the heat beneath it, a heat that bloomed across her back. They both hissed, the burn intensifying. Belphegor moved his hands between and over and around them, muttering something under his breath. She felt like she had been laid inside of a tanning bed, a lamp pressed up against her skin directly between her shoulder blades.

"Repeat after me," Acheron whispered now. She nodded. "I am yours as I am mine."

"I am yours as I am mine."

"You are mine as you are yours."

"You are mine as you are yours."

The heat hit its plateau then, and they each shuddered. Belphegor placed his hand over hers on Acheron's chest, still speaking quietly in a language she could not identify. Then all at once, the heat and pain were gone, and when Belphegor removed her hand, the mark was gone too. Although...

She traced the place where it had been with her fingers. She could still feel it under his flesh. Reaching back to touch hers, she just dusted the top of her own mark, which was not a deep wound but a patch of raised skin.

"Did it work?" she asked.

Belphegor looked to Acheron. Acheron was looking at her. Then he took her hand.

"Let's find out."

15

PENELOPE

She came to with a gasp, bolting upright in bed and looking around the room. She knew by the look of things that she was awake and away from Hell, and she immediately threw the covers back from her body.

"Acheron?"

His name was softer than a pin drop coming off of her tongue as if she feared something might shatter, or shatter her. But he didn't appear. He didn't materialize in a corner. He wasn't there.

"Acheron?"

Nothing. Seconds passed. Then minutes. She inhaled deeply, focused. She closed her eyes, screwing them tight enough to see stars. Then she tugged. Not something in her hands but something wrapped around her soul.

Acheron.

She opened her eyes, the stars twinkling in front of her. She blinked once, twice, three times. Then there he was, standing before her in the flesh, grinning.

"Sorry, Bel was - tailoring the suit," he explained sheepishly.

She grinned too. "Well, let's see it."

He chuckled. "I have it on, Princess."

"What?" Her face fell. "No, you don't."

"I do, but you see me as you want to see me. If your sister were to walk in here right now, she would see someone human. That's how it works. You know my true form. You accepted it."

She wet her lips. "Yeah, I did... But I still wanna know what my sister is gonna be looking at."

He rolled his eyes but shut them soon after. It was truly just to see it all, every facet of him, to know he was real. He blurred before her, his form shrinking and shifting until it was no longer her demon standing before her but a man. A man with dark brown skin, jet black hair in tight curls atop his head, and a thick beard lining his jaw. She looked him over, admiring the look. He was indeed handsome, her Acheron still evident in his eyes, and her sister would certainly approve. As would her mother. But they weren't here at the moment.

She waved her hand.

"Very impressive. Bel does good work. Great work even. But..."

"But what?"

"I'd like my demon back now."

The excitement lit up his face as if he hadn't actually expected her to mean what she had said before, and in a single blink of her eyes, he stood in all his hellish glory once more. She jumped into his arms, and he caught her of course, their foreheads falling together and that cord between them going taut.

"I can feel it," she whispered, more to herself than to him. "Like - a tether."

"That's exactly what it is. A tether. And a door."

"A door?"

"Yes. We know all of each other now. I don't just feel what you feel. I understand it. I understand what it means to be human."

"So - I'll understand what it means to be a demon?"

He smirked. "You've always been a little bit of a demon, naughty girl." She rolled her eyes, but he went on. "You can move freely through the world, and I can too, but getting back to you is already written." He took her hand in his, causing her to look up at him. "But, Penelope, just know that - if you ever - you know, find someone else you want to be with, you can tell me. I will still protect you, still keep you safe. This is a security if nothing else, so—"

"Acheron, I don't want anyone else. I'm not going to want anyone else."

"You can't possibly know that. But loving you alone will keep me warm at night, and if you choose at the end of your life not to be with me physically, I will still make sure your life here is pleasant."

She shook her head, a sad smile on her face. It was an odd thing to see a demon insecure, but he had no need to worry. She would spend the rest of her days proving that to him.

"So - I haven't changed at all?" she pondered. "I mean, I'm still mortal, still human, still getting old every single day."

"Yes, but what does that matter?"

"I don't know. I guess I expected..."

"Immortality?" She nodded. He snickered. "Binding the soul is only a tether. That's why it's reversible. Giving the soul is different."

"Why couldn't I do that?"

He barked a laugh, his eyes glittering with mirth. "Still a needy girl."

"And I'm not ashamed of it."

He ran a hand through her hair. "Let's give this a test run first, hm? You still have time to make that decision, but for now, let us do this. Let us learn to navigate this - very odd and new and freeing relationship. If you decide in a few year's time you still want to, I will have it arranged. Now that we're bound, the process is very simple. Just one more step, and—"

"What is it?"

His grin was so wide that she feared his face would crack in two, but he simply tapped her nose with his finger before leaning down for a kiss.

"Patience, my love," he hissed against her mouth. "We have better things to do with our time at the moment, don't you think?"

She wanted to ask again, to insist, and she knew that he knew that, but she allowed him to lay her down on the mattress and undress her anyway, taking his time peeling each layer of fabric from her skin. It felt different here in the waking world, each sensation more potent and prevalent, the weight of her feelings for him heavier although they made her feel so much lighter than ever before.

"What are you thinking about?" he asked, kneeling between her thighs.

"Can't you read them?"

He shook his head slowly. "Here in the waking world, I can only hear what is meant for me now that we are bound. It is a sign of respect."

"I have nothing to hide from you." She licked her lips. "—Can I hear yours?"

He nodded this time. "We can speak to one another now,

like that, no matter where we are. So even when I am away from you, I am always in reach."

"That is a huge relief because I would hate to have to drag you up here every time I want to talk to you."

His lips curled. "I wouldn't mind."

Leaning down, he kissed a path up her belly, through the valley of her breasts, up along her neck. A soft groan left her, her hands moving up his neck to his antlers.

"Go slow," she whispered. "I want to savor it."

"Mm, we'll see how long that lasts for us."

When he sunk into her now, it was such an odd sensation although not in a bad way whatsoever. His cock felt slim and narrow, nothing like what she knew it to be, but it began to inflate once it was inside, filling her up the way she had become accustomed to. She responded with a sigh of deep pleasure, grinding her hips up into him. Her need for him was palpable, realer than anything else in the room, and she inhaled it like the sweetest drug.

"We have to be much more careful now," he hissed, his tongue laving the skin behind her ear.

"Why?"

"We are in your world now. I don't want to destroy your room."

She suddenly fell into a fit of giggles. He raised his head, giving her a questioning look.

"You must feel like - a baby deer right now," she managed through her laughter.

"...Because of my antlers?"

She laughed harder. "No, no, because this is your first time in this realm. You're - brand new, I guess."

"Oh, yeah." He offered a bashful smile. "And I'm sure the outside world will be an adventure, but it's easy here in your room. It - it feels like home."

Her heart swelled, and she pulled him down into a kiss that he deepened with haste. Gradually, it grew rougher until he was moving into her again, her moans pouring into his mouth before her teeth snagged his lower lip. He snarled, bucking his hips into hers which hit her like a bolt of lightning.

"I said - slow," she grunted even as she spread her legs further and reached down to grip what bit of his ass her hands could.

"You started it," he shot back.

"You better finish it."

"With pleasure."

It still didn't take long for him to speed up, for her to beg for more, for him to oblige her. He slipped his hands beneath her legs, pushing her knees towards her chest as he drove into her pussy with the type of thrust that had their hips clapping together and her back arching off of the bed.

"Acheron! Fuck!"

The ability to scream his name was a luxury she never knew she needed, badly too, and it seemed to act as a whip against his backside because it only spurred him on when she shouted it at the Heavens above. The irony was not lost on her, but thoughts of angels and war cries were a long way from her mind. The only assault she could focus on was the one he was putting on her cunt as he propped her ankles on his shoulders and leaned over her further.

Her eyes rolled back, her orgasm shattering every part of her before his kiss pieced it all back together. Her nails scraped against his ass, his back, his hips, anywhere they could reach although they could never quite find perch. Until she managed to grab hold of his tail. It was like flipping a switch, his control all but nonexistent when a strained roar tore out of his throat.

He drew his knees up further, mercy not at all on either of their radars as he rammed into her and her bed rammed into the wall. The frame shrieked almost as loud as she was. She gripped his tail tighter. He took hold of her throat. Their eyes met, steel against steel, the heat between them scorching hot against her skin.

Cum for me. It was the faintest whimper, even in her mind, but he seemed to be hellbent on holding out, and she wasn't going to take that laying down. Well, not entirely. At least not for long. She gave his tail a firm tug, earning another raucous shout that shook the room around them. She wondered what her neighbors would think, if they would be concerned enough to call the police. Yet at the moment, she couldn't find the will to care. What she wanted was to feel him fall to ruin inside of her. And with her next orgasm building at a rapid pace, she was beginning to lose her focus.

Her eyes fluttered shut, but she tugged at his tail again nonetheless. And again and again until he was fucking her so ruthlessly that she feared she would crash right through the headboard, the wall, and right out onto the side lawn. She was almost levitating off of the mattress now, her spine rigid and her muscles spasming. Her free hand was braced against the headboard, both to try and hold it in place and to keep from going headfirst into the wood.

This pussy feels so much better when we're awake. His voice was as light as steam and just as warm, infusing her thoughts and making it almost impossible to concentrate. *I am going to ruin you in this realm and the next, Penelope. I'm gonna fuck you until your body craves only what I can offer. I—*

She was close. So close. Too close. And she needed leverage. With what strength she could muster, she slid her hand up his tail, gripping its end and putting the tip straight into her mouth. His words died on the edge of a strangled yelp as she sucked it down as deep as it would go without making her gag. His claws pierced her throat just enough to draw blood. Her ankles locked behind his neck. Then her vision went white, and all she felt was the white hot and ice cold clash of his cum spraying her walls and spilling out onto the sheets.

She let him pull his tail from her mouth, her own orgasm leaving her completely immobile. It was so much more disorienting when she was awake, the impact of everything he did so much greater. And she loved every bit of it.

He collapsed atop her with a grunt after setting her legs down on either side of him, allowing her to properly sink into the mattress. Her head was swimming, the last dregs of her energy devoted to catching her breath. Every inch of her was pulsing like a million little heartbeats beneath her skin.

Seems like - I'll still be sleeping quite a lot if you're gonna wear me out like this.

She could feel him smirk against her neck. *Perhaps we should limit your -* intake *then.*

You wouldn't dare.

And she wouldn't let him. She knew he knew it too because he let it rest, pressing a soft kiss to her throat. Only then did she force an eye open.

"I'm not gonna start - you know, popping out demon children, am I?"

He snorted, rolling onto his side then his back and taking her with him. "Not a chance. There's a process for it, and—"

She would roll her eyes if she could. "Of course there is."

"We'd need a witch and—"

"Shhh."

She snuggled into him, and he breathed out, wrapping

her up in his arms and wings and blotting out the sun filtering into the room. His scent surrounded her. She'd never noticed him having one before, but he smelled of firewood and some kind of herb she couldn't quite identify. And she loved it.

"I love you." It felt good to say it to him properly.

"And I love you," he replied, his voice light and airy. "I can hardly believe it, but I know I do."

"What does it feel like? For you?"

He sighed, running his hand down her back. "Like I'm whole."

She understood.

Short as their time together had been thus far, it felt like centuries since she'd met him, centuries since she'd shed her fear and watched him bury it on her behalf. She didn't know what came next. She only knew that she wanted to be with him for an eternity even when eternity would never be enough. And whatever came next, a war with hell or high water, she would be ready. *They* would be ready, and they would do whatever needed to be done together.

She relaxed into him and shut her eyes. She was gonna sleep so well tonight.

ACKNOWLEDGMENTS

Thank you everyone for joining me on this new adventure into another series! In fact, Sing Me to Sleep is an introduction to not only one series but a spin-off of that series as well! The first series, debuting in 2022, will focus on the Seven Deadly Sins and their counterparts, the Seven Heavenly Virtues. The second will feature the witches and other creatures that work alongside the Seven Deadly Sins, and this series will feature a little less plot and a lot more (fucking) vibes. I cannot wait to share this new world with you and welcome the Seven to the Virtues Verse. I have been building their lore for over a decade now, and I am excited to finally bring them to life with you all! As always, thank you to my patrons, my fellow authors who have been invaluable comrades in the trenches with me, and all my book reviewers, ARC readers, and book Twitter friends for continually supporting me. I wish I could name you all, but know that if you have ever lent me your support, I appreciate you!

A special thank you to Whit, Nicole, Sil, Ali (Williams), Nick, and Ari. I don't think you all realize just how much you do for me, how you always seem to be there right on time on my worst days to make me laugh or give me guidance or just to remind me I am loved and admired when I need it most. I cannot thank you enough. To Whit, who beta read this book in record time because I was so off schedule that it was wild, and to Sil, who consistently supports and promotes my work and to whom I owe so much of my success to. Thank you all, and I promise that 2022 is going to be even more exciting than 2021!

ALSO BY R.M. VIRTUES

GODS OF HUNGERS

Drag Me Up

Keep Me Close

STANDALONES

What Are the Odds?